MISER'S COPSE

A ghost story

Andrew Bullock

First Edition [December 2019]

ISBN: 9781706478706

First published by Andrew Bullock in December 2019

Instagram: @drewjbullock | Twitter: @andrewjbullock | drewjbullock.wordpress.com

For Peggy, Robert, Eric and Patricia.

To Colin
Hope You Like
Spooky as much as
Sci-Fi !

Anguish is inbred. Once conceived, it will root itself deeply and propagate as thoroughly as it can. Like a trail of bindweed, it will claw and clutch, desperate to remain. When settled, anguish can lay dormant, recumbent, undisturbed; until it decides to slither from its earthy bed, intent on spreading its miserable seed. Despair shall grow, involve and, eventually, consume.

DECEMBER 20TH.

I t was cold.

Verity Tamblyn stood at the bay window of the West London home she shared with her husband, Lochlan. She watched him nimbly climb the stone steps that led from the front door of the house - a terraced Victorian with a basement entrance - a taupe holdall in each of his hands. He disappeared beyond the railings above, where the car was parked on the curb.

Verity's stare rested on the glass of the window - slightly steamed at the edges of each panel, droplets of condensation rolling silently down each pane.

Last Christmas hadn't been so cold; rather mild, in fact. The harsher weather hadn't set in until the new year. But this December had been wickedly raw. Biting.

A chill ran through Verity. She stepped backward, away from the window, hugging herself a little. She was nursing a mug of tea, which she brought to her lips. The warmth from the steam caressed her face comfortingly.

The front door opened with a click, startling her.

Lochlan had returned from the car. He smiled weakly at her and headed across the entranceway, to the staircase that led to their bedroom. He briskly ascended, two steps at a time.

As she watched her husband vanish onto the first floor landing, her gaze rested on the Christmas tree that stood in the corner of the room, next to the staircase. The tree matched the stair banisters, which were adorned with conifer garlands and violet ribbon. The tree was decked plushly – glass cherubs hanging here, North Stars hanging there. These swayed gently and glistened in the white lights that filled the rest of the pine, a plummy sash of ribbon weaving between branches from stem to stern.

Still clutching her mug, Verity walked toward the tree, taking it in. Lochlan had told her not to bother putting it up this year.

"What's the point?" he had asked. "We're not going to be here for *actual* Christmas."

She hadn't listened to him of course, reasoning that they would only be away for a few days, likening him to Ebenezer Scrooge.

She had put it up anyway, one afternoon in late November. This was stupidly early, but she hadn't cared a jot. Lochlan had come home from work, given it one look, glared at her and gone straight upstairs to take one of his overly-long baths, without a word.

"Christmas is about more than just a couple of days," she had said to him later that evening, over supper. "It's about the season."

He had simply rolled his eyes at her - as he so often did.

As Verity stood before her tree, her stare fell onto an ornament: a bundle of sticks, dusted with faux snow. It hung as if placed there by a miniature forester, having collected the wood for his fire. She reached out and took it in her hand as it dangled from the branch. She had bought the ornament last year at a Norwegian Christmas market in Bath on a weekend away in late October.

She had gone with Tammy.

Lochlan returned downstairs from the bedroom with a rucksack flung over his shoulder and his binoculars case under his arm. Hiking and birdwatching: one so athletic, one so torpid. Neither of any interest to Verity.

"This is the last of the stuff," he said. "Except for the turkey pan. Can you bring that out? We're good to go. Ready?"

Verity looked back at the Christmas tree, then at Lochlan.

"Can I finish my tea? I've still got a whole mug-full," she asked.

"Put it in a travel mug when you get the pan from the kitchen," he replied, a tone of impatience in his voice. "We need to get on the road. I'll meet you at the car."

He spun from her and walked toward the front door before stopping, turning back around and clicking his fingers in the direction of the Christmas tree, lit up and looking glorious.

"And don't forget those lights," he said.

Then he left the house.

Verity placed her mug on the bureau and bent down to the power socket behind the tree. She reached for the plug, which always stuck a little. She gave it a pull, without any luck. She tried again, with more force. It was still in place. She grasped at the wire and gave one last tug, letting out a grunt of frustration as she did. The plug came out of the socket, and the tree fell into darkness.

It looked sad, she thought.

⊹⊹⊹

Lochlan had become more affable towards Verity once the journey was underway. Always one for planning and timetables and lists, he had a tendency to turn very curt when he was behind schedule. But he was far more relaxed now that they were in the car, en route. At one point he even moved his hand onto Verity's as she sat in the passenger seat next to him.

The car had warmed her. She continued to clutch her tea - now in a flask - and let the heated leather seats of the roomy vehicle envelope her in molten hot air, as if she were standing with her back to an open oven. She had felt uneasy at home, before they had left; tense and on edge. She had felt doubtful about taking the trip. But now they were on their way, she had already started to relax a little.

This will be good, Verity thought to herself, watching a Toyota overtake them in the fast lane, its wipers whipping across the windscreen violently, despite it only drizzling lightly outside.

Verity looked at her husband as he concentrated on the motorway ahead of him, the low-beam headlights of the oncoming traffic flickering across his chiselled face.

It hadn't been an easy year. Undoubtedly the most taxing twelve months of their five-and-a-half-year marriage. They had always been a somewhat fractious couple, but they had managed to find each other's nuances to be endearing when they had fallen in love. Had they not, they wouldn't ever have made it to the altar. Perhaps, even, they'd have murdered one another halfway down the aisle.

But this year had been unpleasant; almost morose. Stressful and fraught.

Things had begun to unravel last Christmastime. It had started the day after Lochlan's company holiday party. In fact, it had started *at* the party.

They had both attended, of course. Yet Verity had made a mistake. A terrible error of judgement. After it had happened, her husband had been furious with her, finally confronting her about it the following evening when he had returned home from work.

Nonetheless, it had been addressed. She apologised about what had happened, explained the background to it and he had seemingly forgiven her, and moved on.

But he hadn't. Not at all.

As a result, Verity and Lochlan had filled up the rest of last December by taking a stupidly hedonistic approach. They had accepted every invitation to every festive soiree that had come their way: her work party, numerous open houses, his parents' annual, always-tedious, gathering. There was even an event at the local church that they had stumbled upon one Sunday afternoon after devouring a pheasant-for-two at the local pub.

They had needed the distraction.

Christmas Eve had seen the Tamblyns start off with lunch at the Dean Street Townhouse, followed by early evening drinks at one of Lochlan's squash friends' house in Chiswick before completing the evening at Tammy's flat.

It was here that Verity had noticed it - the way her husband scowled at Tammy. He stared at her with a mixture of menace and interest. Knowing now that it was an almost lustful hatred in his eyes, Verity was more attune to this look, ready for if and when it ever crossed Lochlan's face again.

So far, it hadn't.

That Christmas saw her friendship with Tammy come to an abrupt end. But, while the past year had been a healing exercise for her and her husband, the same could not be said for her and Tammy.

They would never heal. Not now.

The roof rack on top of the car clunked above them, startling Verity. Lochlan's eyes flipped upwards at the sound and then rested back on the road ahead of him.

A year on and he seemed to have returned to his former demeanour - no-nonsense, strong-willed, assertive, with deft dashes of softness here and there. Things had certainly become less-strained over the past six months. Still, Lochlan had definitely changed in some ways. He never seemed totally relaxed, and his handsome, normally bright face had become harder. He was a much colder man now, after what both she - and later, he - had done.

Of course everything that had gone wrong over the past year had started when they had clashed over having a child. It was something Lochlan so craved, and the burden weighed down on Verity's shoulders like a stone gable; partially because she had so far been unable to give him a baby, but greatly because she wasn't sure she actually *wanted* one. She didn't know. As flippant as that sounded, it was the truth.

It might have been that she was simply not ready yet. But this indecisiveness did not wash well with her husband. He was a planner. He knew what he wanted. He expected the same from those around him. There was nothing vague or flowery about Lochlan.

He yawned. Even his yawn was assertive and direct; purposeful and in no way slovenly.

"Tired?" Verity asked him, suddenly aware that the light had dropped sufficiently and the sun was now a lot lower, closing in on the rooftops of whatever town they were passing.

"Why? Do *you* want to drive?" Lochlan answered, his lips curling into a playful smirk.

Verity let out a little laugh.

"You know the answer to that," she said, shifting in her seat a little.

He knew; he knew that she hated driving his car with a passion. It was big and over-complicated and clunky. Why he needed a Land Rover in London was beyond Verity. But then, once in a blue moon, they'd take a trip like this and he'd be able to justify it.

"You watch how she manoeuvres when we get to Fallows' Spinney," he insisted, referring to the machine as a "her" as always did.

His second wife.

"We're spending Christmas in a cottage on the outskirts of a village in the countryside. We're hardly going off-roading on the glaciers," Verity teased, turning to gaze out of the passenger window.

"The key word there was *outskirts*," Lochlan said, taking his eyes off the road momentarily to look at his wife. "The place we're staying is pretty desolate. It's a mile or so from the village. The terrain could be rough."

"You *hope* the terrain will be rough," Verity teased, looking back at Lochlan once more.

Her eyes met his; just for a second.

Cautious as ever, he promptly returned his concentration back to the road, with a slant of a smile on his face.

She was smiling, too.

Verity was woken by the quietness.

She had fallen asleep back on the M5, as the light had become dimmer and the sound of the passing traffic had sunken into a distant continuous hum. Their car had been travelling at the same steady speed for the entire time it had been on the motorway, and this seemed to have sent Verity into a doze.

Now, however, the road was craggier. The smooth tarmac of the motorway was long behind them and Lochlan was driving along a country lane. Outside it was dark, save for the gleam of their car headlights illuminating the narrow road in front.

"Are we there?" Verity asked, sitting up from her slouched position in the cosy seat.

"Almost, yeah," Lochlan replied, eyes locked ahead of him.

Verity stretched out a little - one perk of having an unnecessarily huge vehicle - and squinted at the road through the windshield. They were driving underneath a canopy of oak trees that lined each side of the lane. The branches - russety leaves clinging on to them still, having not yet given in to the barren season - met in the middle above them. The boughs were so thick that, despite it being midwinter, it was difficult to see any sky through them.

Verity leant forward and looked up through the windshield, making out that the sun had yet to fully set, leaving an eerie orangey-charcoal sky seeping through the sparse breaks in the trees.

"How long was I asleep?" Verity asked Lochlan.

"Not long. I guess, fifty minutes," he replied. "We came off the motorway just before Worcester and went through Malvern Hills. Now we're heading west, through the foothills. That's where the forest starts and where Fallows' Spinney is."

Verity tutted.

"Fallows' Spinney. It's not very Christmassy," she remarked.

Lochlan waited a few seconds. Keeping his eyes on the road,

he held back from responding to his wife's last remark.

"What does *that* mean?" he asked her, eventually.

"What?" she replied.

"That comment about it being Christmassy," he elaborated.

She didn't reply to this.

"Was that another dig?" he pressed.

Verity glared at her husband, his face gloomy in the evening light, the blue dashboard controls reflecting slightly across his hardened gaze as he scrutinised the lane ahead.

"Seriously Lochlan?" Verity exhaled with annoyance. "You're not honestly going to start this now are you?"

"No," he retorted. "But Verity, you just made a dig."

"Christ. No I didn't," she insisted. "You need to stop taking everything I say so literally. The place we're going doesn't have a very festive name, that's all. It's true - it doesn't."

"Ah, so I should have purposefully found somewhere with a name like Winterborough or Mistletoe-On-Thames or Santa's fucking Grotto?"

There was a tremor in his voice as he said this. When they jibed at one another, it always happened so suddenly, just like this.

"Don't be ridiculous," Verity replied. "That's not what I meant."

"I know you didn't want to go away for Christmas," Lochlan went on. "But can we drop the snide remarks while we're here. You know I booked this for our benefit. This is for us."

"I didn't mean anything by it!" Verity declared, a tint of hysteria in her voice.

"Okay!"

Lochlan dropped it, and continued to look firmly over the steering wheel ahead of him. Verity folded her arms and slumped back, glancing out of the window.

This happened a lot. One minute they were fine - content, jovial, comfortable. The next, one comment would be blown out of proportion and they'd be having a tiff. But not a silly quarrel about something trivial; their tiffs were strenuous and anarchic.

The car had passed out from under the canopy of trees and was now moving along a straight narrow lane, stone walls on either side of the track, ploughed frost-tinged fields beyond each one. Beyond these were more fields, stretching out for miles in the dusky light. Ahead of them, a mass of woodland seemed to rise from the horizon, as if it had rapidly sprouted from the earth there and then. Verity looked on as the jagged horde of trees got nearer, the car's lights, now on full-beam, illuminating the thick, dark trunks. Then, just as abruptly as the wood had materialised, the Land Rover dropped briskly. A dip in the road - not marked by any signage - forced the car to descend suddenly as the lane wound down a steep sag, leading directly into the forest.

Verity gasped a little, feeling her stomach drop as the car went into the dip, grabbing onto the dashboard in front of her. Lochlan shot her a look of disdain, clearly finding her overly-dramatic. She ignored him, keeping her eyes on road in front, watching the lane as the car moved along it.

The lane seemed to be getting leaner and leaner and there was nothing to be seen either side of it thanks to the trees of the forest they were now driving through. The woodland was dense, and what little there was left of the daylight was totally obstructed. It was as if the car had dropped, literally, into the undergrowth, and that the open land and the vast sky was now way above them, on another plain of existence.

Eventually the road widened once more, and the thick trees that so suffocatingly encroached on them started to disperse a little. Ahead, illuminated by the car's lights, a wooden sign leaned slightly out into the lane.

"Fallows' Spinney - 1 mile," read the faded white lettering.

After a minute or two more of driving, the occasional stone-built cottage started to appear on the sides of the lane; and before long, the road had wound to a forked junction. To the right, the road continued to widen, and more houses could be seen, windows lit-up here and there, the occasional wisp of wood smoke snaking upwards from a chimney, twinkling Christmas lights strewn across a couple of bare trees. Beyond this, there were further buildings, all built in the same style: stony, crooked and aged. The last of the orange sunlight reflected off the black flint roofs. A church spire could be seen in the distance, and from it a bell struck five times.

"Five O Clock. We're right on schedule," Lochlan said, satisfied with his planning.

To the left, the woodland continued, and the lane became narrower again, continuing to weave through the trees. A post stood between the fork in the road that read "Fallows' Spinney" with an arrow pointing right towards the village of stone houses, and another pointing left with the lettering "Miser's Copse".

A Christmas wreath hung from the sign. It was beautiful – plush and green, made with fir, sprigs of juniper berry, some trailing ivy and silver birch twigs. Somehow, Verity was comforted by it. It was welcoming but, for some reason, eerily so.

Lochlan turned the steering wheel sharply to the left, veering the car onto the track marked "Miser's Copse". This was where the cottage they were renting for the week was situated. Lochlan had chosen it because it wasn't in the midst of the village. It was close enough to wander in, take lunch at the local pub, potter around any of the quaint little shops that were bound to be there; but he and Verity would still very much have their privacy.

The car drove through the trees, the road once again plunged into canopied darkness, on another steep decline. A few minutes later, the woodland cleared, and Verity and Lochlan found themselves on an open road, moors stretching out on either side, shrouded in a low-clinging mist, the occasional snaggy-looking tree poking up here and there.

Ahead of them was their cottage. It was surrounded by a stone wall, which encircled the front garden, reminiscent of a tomb-less churchyard. Brambles crept over the wall from the cottage garden and moss was dotted along the tips of it, damp in the December evening air. There was a paint-chipped gate leading into a small gravelled courtyard driveway, where the back entrance to the cottage was.

Beyond the cottage, across the moor and uphill, Verity could see a cluster of trees - the copse that the place was named after. The trees were mostly bare-branched and some even looked to be dead. The odd pine stood among them, thick with evergreen boughs. Hawthorne bushes lay close to the ground encircling the copse, which was fairly large - more of a miniature wood. It was thick enough to walk into and disappear. It stood alone, in the middle of the moor - solitary, dark and uninviting.

✠✠✠

The inside of the cottage was surprisingly out of tune with everything else Verity had seen of Fallows' Spinney and Miser's Copse since they had arrived. And she was rather relieved.

Lochlan had already collected the key from the letting office in Belgravia that morning, so they had been able to get inside straight away. This had pleased Verity, who had felt the chill of the heathland surrounding the property as soon as she had stepped out of the cosy Land Rover and onto the wet, pebbly driveway.

Above the cottage door the name of the property had been engraved into the wood. Blink, and you'd miss it altogether. Scratched in unruly scrawl were the words "The Spinney House".

Inside was surprisingly modern. It looked to have been renovated in recent months. Everything was in mint condition, barely a mark on any of the walls or a scratch on any of the surfaces. The door from the courtyard driveway opened into a cramped ante-room. It was panelled with stained Maplewood and offered a place to hang coats, dry out umbrellas and store firewood. Lochlan lead Verity inside and shut the door behind them, dropping their bags to the ground.

"It smells nice," was Lochlan's first observation.

He was right; there was a scent of polish merged with what reminded her of baked apples.

They went through the door that lead from the porch into the kitchen. It was still small and cottage-like, yet thoroughly contemporary. The walls were painted in a deep indigo shade, with plum skirting. The floors were mahogany and the worktops and surfaces were a combination of matte steel and dark walnut. The appliances and fixtures all looked brand new - stainless steel, glistening in the trio of industrial halogen lights that hung in a row above the kitchen's central island. A table and chairs sat to the right of the space, a damask runner sweeping the centre of the table top. On it stood two tall iron candelabras, each sporting a violet-coloured wick. Between them, in the centre of the table, was a glorious white poinsettia.

At least they've tried to make it Christmassy, Verity thought to herself, looking at the triangular creamy petals of the flower.

To her astonishment, however, the owners of The Spinney House had done more than simply invest in a seasonal pot plant. On entering the room beyond the kitchen, Lochlan and Verity were met with a stunningly furnished living area - breathtakingly decorated for the Christmas holiday.

Again, not large in size, the room boasted thick, warming curtains that hung majestically from rails attached to the beamed ceilings and furnishings upholstered with an orange and grey pattern of vine leaves, positioned around a large stone fireplace, stocked with birch wood. The mantle was strung with a garland of pine, woven with silver birch bark and dotted here and there with sprigs of bay leaf.

In the corner of the room stood a large Norway spruce, filled with ornaments in an eye-catching design of apricot and bronze. Thick satin ribbon snaked from the bottom of the tree to the top, meeting a regal-looking angel statuette at the tree's summit, made from brass wire.

As Verity took in the room, she felt Lochlan step up beside her and place his arm around her waist.

"That's quite a Christmas tree," he observed.

Verity smiled to herself. She noted a hint of smugness in her husband's voice. But above all, he seemed content. As was she.

╬╬╬

Lochlan and Verity made love that evening. It was only the second time they had done so that December. The last time had been after a dinner party they had attended with a couple of friends, where they had all overdone it on cranberry vodka spritzers.

They had argued on the way home that night over something trivial and had ended up locked in a passionate tangle on the kitchen counter. It hadn't really been love-making - more a form of pent-up unbridling that had manifested itself into an alcohol-infused paroxysm.

In other words: it was hate sex. But Lochlan and Verity did not hate each other.

Now, for the first time in a long time, they made love tenderly at The Spinney House. It had been blissful.

Yet, once they had finished, and Lochlan was lying in the spacious bed of the master bedroom, his chest moving slowly with the rhythm of his sleep, Verity felt a chill. It was the same chill she had felt at their living room window at home that afternoon, as she had watched her husband go to and from the car.

She lay beside him, watching him, listening to him breathe. And from nowhere, she felt as if she were about to cry.

She didn't - instead dabbing each eye with the back of her hand, briskly turning over on her pillow, away from her husband.

DECEMBER 21ST.

Lochlan was up early. He was a morning person. Verity wasn't.

He liked to give her grief about this; but they were on holiday now, and it was the week of Christmas. She was there to rest and relax. She was there to feel at ease with Lochlan and with herself.

He left her a note, which Verity awoke to find on the pillow next to her.

It read:

> *"Weather's beautiful. Gone to Fallows' Spinney for supplies. Didn't want to wake you. Be back soon. L."*

It was quite a statement that Lochlan had left the note beside Verity in the bed. She would have presumed him to leave it in the kitchen, on the worktop, so that she would have woken up wondering where he was, not finding out until she'd gone downstairs.

It was the sex, Verity thought to herself as she sat up in bed. The sex had lifted his mood.

It was at this point she remembered how sombre she had felt, lying next to him after they had made love. But, as the sun streamed through their small bedroom window, bathing the room in a glorious golden light, she decided not to dwell on unsettling feelings from the evening before.

She got out of bed and grabbed the cardigan that she had draped over the back of the dressing table chair. As she straightened it out to put it on, she glanced at her reflection in the mirror on the table. There was a scuff mark on her white nightie. She licked her finger and rubbed at it, dry flakes of dirt coming off easily. She put on the cardigan and wrapped it closely around her body.

Downstairs, in the kitchen, Verity switched on the coffee percolator - the owners had left the essentials in the house ready for them (coffee grounds, tea, milk and eggs) - and poured herself a glass of water. She took her pill - a mild sedative the doctor had prescribed her in the middle of the year - and set one aside for Lochlan (he took them too) in case he hadn't remembered his before he'd gone out, being that he was in such a good mood.

Once brewed, Verity poured herself a mug of coffee and stood at the window in the kitchen that looked out over the moor, towards Miser's Copse.

Despite being such a clear day, the copse still seemed a little faded in the distance. A low mist clung to the shrubbery that surrounded it. Despite the various birds and occasional sheep that wandered the encircling grassland, the gaggle of trees seemed lifeless and lonesome.

In broad daylight, Verity could see just how densely the trees of the copse grew together. When she had looked up the hill towards it the night before, it had been hard to decipher in the low-light of dusk. But this morning, Miser's Copse looked like a black entangled mass. Actually, it was rather an ugly thing as it broke up the otherwise smooth line of the horizon.

As she took a sip of her coffee Verity noticed, for the first time, movement. She had to squint through the window to double check, but she could see what she thought was an animal, on its hind legs, stood amid the trees at the edge of the copse. It appeared to have antlers. It was a stag, she thought.

Then it moved again, and she realised that it wasn't this at all. It seemed to be a person, lurking in the foliage. The antlers she thought she had seen were merely branches from the tree it was standing in front of. She could see now that it was most definitely a person. A man. Was it Lochlan, she wondered. Had he altered his plans to visit the village and instead trekked up to investigate the wild surrounds? Given that hiking was on his holiday agenda, this would make sense. And besides, the place was so isolated, who else could it be?

The figure moved once more and Verity leaned further forward, trying to decipher whether it was or wasn't her husband. But as she peered intently at the copse, she heard the latch on the driveway gates being unlocked and she turned her head to see Lochlan, stood behind the gates, opening them. The Land Rover was behind him, on the lane, engine running. He had just returned from the village.

Verity looked back toward the copse, and still made out the figure. It was actually much smaller than Lochlan - not a child, just an adult of a shorter build. It didn't move. It was deathly still.

Lochlan drove the car into the driveway, killed the engine and noticed his wife at the window. He gave her a wave and smiled. Verity put down her coffee cup and left the window, heading to the back door that lead to the courtyard.

"You're up. Good. I have breakfast," Lochlan said, stepping out of the car to greet Verity as she left the cottage.

"I am," she said, going to help him with the bags he had with him, pulling her cardigan around her to block out the chill from the crisp December morning.

As she took one of them, she looked beyond the stone perimeter wall, across the moorland. Whatever she had seen was no longer there.

Lochlan clicked shut the boot of the Land Rover and pressed the lock button on his car key, noticing his wife fixated on something over the garden wall, in the distance. He followed her curious stare, toward the copse.

"What?" he asked, simply.

Verity squinted, then shook her head.

"Someone was up there, by those trees," she replied. "I thought it was you, actually."

"Not me," Lochlan said, heading to the cottage door. "A farmer?"

"Probably," Verity said, glancing over at the sodden frost-tipped sheep that stood in the meadows, chewing lazily on chunks of green grass.

┼╍╂╍┼

Verity had been surprised at Lochlan's lack of insistence to go for a walk, or a drive, or - anything.

He had clearly understood that not only was it Christmas-time, but he was on holiday. There were no last minute trips to Oxford Street to be done, to desperately scour Marks & Spencer for the pair of fur-lined gloves his mother had wanted that he had forgotten to buy. No panic over the realisation that he had ordered a turkey stuffed with sage and lemon rather than rosemary and onion, rendering cousin Marilyn unable to eat any thanks to the citric allergies she supposedly had after that incident with the orange face cream. No arguments over whether or not they would be going to his mother's or her mother's for a pre-Christmas sherry on Christmas Eve. None of the seasonal trivialities of life in London.

So, they had a fairly lazy day. They were alone, together, in the middle of a remote moor, tucked away from the world in a charming country cottage.

Lochlan was the joint-owner of a company that designed and produced climbing equipment for mountaineers; and, with the troubles in their marriage over the past year, he had thrown himself into his work more so than usual. After what had been a taxing twelve months, both emotionally and physically, he was due a rest.

She was too. Verity worked for a wallpaper designer. It was a highbrow company who were hired by esteemed interior decorators to adorn the homes of socialites. It wasn't quite as de-

21

manding as Lochlan's job, but it had been a busy year for the company nonetheless. She had been thankful to know that she could dissipate her woes with her work.

Lochlan was quite content reclining on the plush sofa in the living room that afternoon, having enjoyed both breakfast and lunch made up of fare from the local village - croissants from the bakers for breakfast, fresh goose foie gras from the butchers for lunch. He sat and scrutinised his crossword as Verity knelt by the Christmas tree and placed the gifts that they had brought for one another around the trunk.

The clock above the mantle struck four as she repositioned the smallest-sized present she had bought for her husband neatly in front of one of his larger gifts. She looked towards the living room window, which offered views over the front garden, and the lane beyond the wall that lead back into the larger forest and Fallows' Spinney. It had become more overcast that afternoon, and the temperature had dropped suddenly around noon. Grey clouds hung low over the tops of the forest trees in the distance and night-time was drawing in earlier than usual. The crescent moon could be seen through the cloud, blue-tinted and icy.

There was a tap at the door.

Not the side door through the kitchen, but the front door in the living room, where they were both spending the afternoon. Lochlan looked up from his crossword, in the direction of the knock.

"I didn't hear a car, did you?" he asked Verity, who stayed knelt at the foot of the tree.

"No," she replied, shaking her head.

Lochlan tossed his newspaper onto the coffee table and stood up. He rubbed at the side of his neck as he walked across the room to the front door and opened it.

From her position beneath the Christmas tree, Verity couldn't see beyond the door, which was made from heavy oak and only had a small circular window in it, too high and too small to see who was behind it. So thick was the door that she could barely hear what was being said, let alone be able to decipher who had knocked at it, disturbing their comfortable and rather serene winter's afternoon.

After the visitor had mumbled something, Lochlan replied, much louder than whoever he was talking to. Verity made out something along the lines of, "that's kind, but I think we're okay," followed by, "yes, I'm sure. But Merry Christmas to you," after which the faint voice of the visitor could be heard saying a final few words before shuffling off down the garden path.

Lochlan closed the front door and turned to Verity, shooting her a slightly amused yet baffled look.

"That was weird."

"What? Who was it?"

"Some guy. A man. A really small old guy. Trying to flog me firewood."

Verity scrunched her nose up at this. "On his own?"

"Yes. No one else was out there. No one I saw anyway."

Lochlan walked back to the sofa and sunk back down into it, taking up his crossword and pencil again.

"It's getting dark," Verity observed, looking again out of the living room window. "And it's cold. And we're in the middle of nowhere."

"I know," Lochlan replied, his concentration focused again on his puzzle.

"And no car? He didn't drive here?" Verity checked.

"Nope."

Verity tutted at her husband. "You could have at least bought some wood off him," she scolded.

Lochlan glanced up at her. "Why?"

"Some old guy turns up here, made the trip to the cottage, probably heard there were people staying here, and you sent him off without buying one log?"

"I don't have any cash on me."

Verity rolled her eyes.

"He's probably still out there, lurking on the lane if you want to try and catch him," Lochlan said, uninterestedly. "Maybe he'll take a credit card. He looked like he doesn't know what an iPad is, but you never know."

Verity placed another present at the foot of the tree and stood up. "I'm going to make some coffee. Do you want some?"

Lochlan shook his head. "No. Thank you," he said, letting his eyes drop back down to his newspaper.

She left him and walked into the kitchen, re-filled the coffee machine with a new filter and fresh grounds and waited for it to brew. The machine gurgled and spluttered as she strolled over to the front kitchen window that overlooked the lane leading to Fallows' Spinney.

The light was low, but she could still see the road clearly. No one was out there. Had the man been elderly, and on foot, surely he would still be visible heading back towards the village, Verity deduced.

She then had a thought, and turned to walk to the other kitchen window - the one she had been at earlier that morning, looking out at Miser's Copse. This side of the house was a lot darker, and a low haze had already begun to creep across the moor beyond the garden wall.

There he was: the figure of a man - small, lean, hunched over - walking across the heath. This had to be their visitor.

Was this who she had seen in the morning, standing up at the edge of the trees, Verity wondered? Was The Spinney House not as solitary as they had presumed?

DECEMBER 22ND.

L ochlan had been off-hand with Verity following the remarks about the man at the door. She had, in turn, realised that she should have kept quiet and that there was no room for petty disagreement while they were away for Christmas. As ridiculous as this sounded, things were still too fragile to bicker about such trivialities; and as a peace offering Verity had given her husband one of the gifts under the tree, despite Christmas being three days away.

This had perked him up. It was a vintage copper keyring that he had seen a few weeks ago in a shop on Yeoman's Row and had expressed a particular interest in. Verity had been sure to return and buy it the week before their trip, knowing he'd be pleased.

In a deliberate attempt to continue to keep the peace, Verity had then suggested Lochlan spend the following morning hiking on the heath, and that they would go to the village later that afternoon, where they would stay for dinner.

He left at dawn, and Verity watched from the bedroom window as her husband began his trek across the moor, south, away from the cottage, the forest and the copse.

It had been unlike her to not fall immediately back into bed and enjoy another few hours to herself; but Verity was too awake, alert and a little on edge. It occurred to her that she had really done very little with herself since they had arrived at The Spinney House, and that she was looking forward to getting out and visiting Fallows' Spinney later that afternoon.

After breakfast she took a stroll around the walled garden. It was quite small, especially compared to the vast moorland that surrounded the property. It was unkempt - but charmingly so. Wild roses grew on the south-side of the cottage and an old well sat at the end of the garden, tatty and unusable, but winsome all the same.

Then there was the small coal store by the wall that ran along the back-end of the garden. The coal store was also ramshackle, and Verity strolled over to it and kicked at some of the remnant coal that was littered around the mouth of the brick structure. She shuffled bits of the charred black rock tidily into the little hole with her foot as she gazed casually out at the fields beyond the garden, a murder of crows dancing in the sky above.

By mid-morning, Verity had phoned her mother, washed up the breakfast things and tidied up the slight mess Lochlan had left in the bedroom having gotten ready in the dark earlier on. She had then found herself on the armchair by the hearth with her book, but had barely read three sentences before she had drifted into a doze.

A scratching noise awoke her.

At first, she presumed Lochlan was back and rummaging in the kitchen; but as she came out of her light nap, she realised that it was coming from the front door, across the living room.

Verity glanced at her watch. It was noon.

She placed her book - which had fallen into her lap as she had dozed off - onto the side table and stood up, frowning at the door, trying to decipher the sound.

It was certainly a scratching of some sort, as if a briar was brushing against the doorframe in the wind. But there were no vines or branches anywhere near the front door, and this was particularly consistent.

Verity shrugged, and walked across the living room. It was the middle of the day; she wasn't afraid.

She reached for the handle and pulled open the heavy cottage door as briskly as her petite build could manage. In doing so, she startled the man standing on the doorstep - who in turn startled her.

He was shorter than her, by around a foot or so. He wore faded grey and beige clothing - trousers that looked as if they had once been smart but were now very worn; a yellowing shirt, tucked in beneath a knitted grey sweater, mostly hidden by a blazer jacket, the odd hole in the fabric at the elbows. He also had a woollen scarf wrapped around his throat, chequered in pattern but faded over time, the ends frazzled.

His hair was grey, with flecks of auburn here and there - the colour it must have once been all over. His skin was pallid - presumably due to the winter air. His lips were cracked and slightly blue-tinged. White whiskers sprouted here and there from his chin. His complexion was waxen and creased, his eyes sunken and rather bloodshot.

At first, he frightened Verity; the shock of finding someone lurking on her doorstep combined with his unhealthy appearance had taken her aback. He had looked at her with a glare at first, which had caused a shiver to shoot through her body. But after a second, his hollow cheeks and cloven lips had morphed into a smile. It was a smile of friendliness - but Verity found it impossible to decipher whether or not it was forced or unfeigned.

Regardless, she smiled back.

"You startled me, I'm so sorry," she said, placing a hand to her chest in mock-relief.

"I apologise," the man said, his voice raspy and aged. "I had hoped not to disturb you."

Verity looked at his hands - on which he wore fingerless taupe gloves - and realised he was holding a hammer and nail. She looked back up at her visitor's grinning face, still unsure of him.

"I wanted to wish you the best of the season, and surprise you with a gift," the man said, nodding to the doorstep.

Verity followed his gaze and noticed a freshly-made wreath, propped up against the step. It was beautifully constructed - intricate and ornate. It was fashioned with moss and cedar, decorated with sprigs of huckleberry, crab-apple and rosehip.

"This is for me?" Verity asked. "For us?"

The man smiled at her again. He had no teeth, save for one, yellowed and jagged.

"Yes," he said, nodding. "I had wanted to fix it to your door quietly, as a gift. A surprise."

Verity bent down and picked up the wreath, admiring it carefully in her hands.

"You made this yourself?" she asked, looking up, her eyes meeting his, which were creased at the sides by his fixed grin.

"Yes," he nodded. "But it's a gift. I had hoped you wouldn't hear me if I tapped the nail lightly into the wood. I wanted it to be a surprise. 'Tis the season for such frivolity, after all."

Verity smiled at the man, and asked: "Are you from the village?"

A slight look of concern flashed briefly over his face.

"This is something I like to do," he said, not answering her question. "Just for a few locals."

"It really is lovely," Verity said, running one finger over the soft moss of the wreath.

"I had not wanted to disturb you," the man insisted again, suddenly frowning rather deeply. "After yesterday."

He didn't elaborate. Verity watched him, his reddened eyes travelling down to the ground.

"Oh," she said, now realising who he was. "Were you the gentleman selling firewood yesterday?"

His eyes flew back up to meet hers.

"Yes. The young man -"

"My husband."

"Yes. He declined."

Verity felt sorry for her visitor. A sudden wave of disdain swept over her, towards Lochlan. This man was old and looked practically destitute. How could he refuse him, and at Christmastime too?

"Let me pay you for this beautiful wreath," Verity asserted. "Please. I really do insist."

The man looked stunned at the offer and held up both his gloved hands, hammer and nail still clasped in one.

"No. *No.*"

"Please, let me offer you something."

"I can't," he said, almost panicked. "It's my way of saying season's greetings to you."

Verity didn't know what to say. She didn't want to insult him further by forcing money into his frail, frozen hands when he had tried to surprise her with this gesture.

"I'm sorry about my husband," was all she could think to say next.

The man stared at her, his eyes examining her face carefully.

"If you'd like, perhaps you'd be interested in some of my other items," he suggested, slowly, gesturing to the lane beyond the cottage gates.

Verity glanced beyond the old man and noticed a small wooden cart - a little like a wheelbarrow, but that one pulls rather than pushes. It was filled with various cuttings of ivy, boughs of fir, pine cones, bunches of seasonal flowers and clumps of berries.

"If you'd like, I have things to decorate your cottage with," the man said. "I have a garland for the stairs and plenty of other things. A sprig of mistletoe, to ensure a kiss on Christmas Day."

Verity found the last remark to be somewhat obscure. He said it with an odd certainty - a knowingness in his ruddy-looking eyes. It was rather close to home, she felt; almost as if this man knew that she and Lochlan could easily go through that Christmas without even a hug, based on the last twelve months. They may very well have made love, but there was still three days to fall out before Christmas Day would be upon them.

Yet she shrugged off the remark, and smiled warmly.

"I'd love to buy some of your things, yes. We're only renting the cottage and it could do with some Christmas decorations actually, there aren't many in there," she lied, sure to pull the door a little more closed behind her so as to block any view of the brightly-lit regal-looking tree that stood in the corner by the staircase.

The man beamed thinly and suggested she take her pick from the cart while he finished hanging the wreath to the front door. She left him to his task and perused the selection out on the lane, all the while considering how difficult this elderly man of apparent ill health must have found it to pull the cart along the rickety lanes of Fallows' Spinney.

Consequently, she was sure to pick several of his goods, more than enough for the house - an amount that would be sure to lighten his load. She had a £50 note in her purse, which she offered to him, telling him she would also take some firewood, as they were bound to run out.

He didn't argue with her, and was clearly glad of her generosity, helping her with the various garlands and sprigs of greenery that she selected, as well as a few logs for the fire, before giving one final glance at the wreath he had hung and thanking her.

"Season's greetings to you and your husband," he said with a nod as he turned from Verity and hobbled back up the garden path to the gate.

Then he stopped. Abruptly.

Verity didn't speak, but watched from the doorway.

Slowly, the man turned around to face her again. He was smiling - but there was something much colder about this smile. It was more of an unsavoury grin. It was sinister. His eyes were dark all of a sudden, and he looked at her with a macabre fascination. It was enough to prompt Verity to place a hand on the door in an attempt at support or comfort.

After a moment, the old man spoke again.

"You killed her."

He said it with a distorted piquancy; his tone was nastily joyful. It was enough to prompt a look of distress on Verity's face, clearly visible to the man stood before her.

His expression didn't soften, but he spoke again with a kinder manner: "Don't fret. You were right to kill her."

Those words: "kill her". They rang in Verity's ears like a vicious wasp, wickedly buzzing around her head. So dumbfounded by this sudden turn in both the man's character and the topic of conversation, Verity remained frozen in place on the step, glad to be holding on to the doorframe. She clutched it tighter, her hand grasping onto the oak.

The man frowned at Verity - a look of concern; not for her wellbeing, but as a response to her shock. It was as if he was troubled that she had disagreed with him.

You were right to kill her.

So, he turned and walked off, up the path, back toward his cart.

Verity closed her eyes.

She felt hot, despite the cold afternoon air on her face. She inhaled slowly, processing what had just been said to her. Her head swam a little. She needed a moment or two.

When she opened her eyes, however, the man and his cart were gone.

✝∙✝∙✝

After the man had seemingly vanished from the path, Verity had hastily locked the door and stood at the front window of the cottage for quite some time. She supposed she had been keeping an eye out for this person - this pedlar, or whoever he was - in case he came back. She would have in fact liked to speak further to him, and would have asked him to explain himself. Or perhaps she would have stayed indoors, and just watched him from the window, happier knowing where he was. But he didn't return and it unnerved her.

She glanced at her watch. It was One O Clock. Lochlan should've been home by now, she thought.

She waited at the window a little longer, staring out at the lane beyond the garden wall, in the direction of the forest they had driven through two days before. It looked more jagged and unruly in the flat afternoon light. Clouds had formed above the surrounding fens and Verity suddenly felt enclosed, oppressed. She became more agitated on her own, indoors, and wished that

Lochlan would return from his hike so that they could go into the village and experience something other than utter solitude.

Fifteen minutes later she relocated to the kitchen, where she fingered the "on" switch of the coffee percolator before abandoning all thoughts of caffeine, instead opting for the chilled chardonnay that was beckoning her from the fridge.

She poured herself a glass and sat on one of the stools that lined the kitchen counter, nursing her drink and staring vacantly across the room, her mind wandering.

You killed her.

She could not expel the words from her mind. She wanted to brush it off as a coincidence, but it seemed impossible. The way the man had said it - it had seemed threatening to her. Perhaps she was paranoid, but the undeniable change in his temperament had been quite startling.

He had frightened her.

She sipped from her glass of wine and shut her eyes, feeling the cool alcohol trickle down her dry throat. She thought of the man on the path, staring at her. She seemed to remember him differently, in hindsight. Almost a darker figure, not altogether real. His hollow eyes piercing her, his macabre grin snaking across his crusted lips. She now looked at this small, hunched over figure as something unsettling; a dark and penetrating presence that had watched her from the gate before saying those stinging words.

She opened her eyes again, suddenly afraid to not be totally alert. She glanced nervously toward the kitchen windows, half-expecting the pedlar to be stood at one of them, peeking in at her malevolently.

Why had he said it? How could he have known about it? About *"her"*?

Verity's mind was racing, desperate for some form of logic. She looked through the door, back into the living room, where she had left the Christmas garlands and other items she had bought from the man who had turned up unannounced and created this unwanted flurry of anguish with just three words.

32

You killed her.

She did not want his goods in her home. A rush of disdain swept over her and she hopped off her stool, placed the wine glass on the table as she marched past it and into the living room, sweeping one of the garlands up in her arms. She walked toward the front door, eager to remove all traces of this person from the house.

She reached for the handle and threw open the door - the cold air hitting her. The sun had all but vanished through the bank of clouds above the cottage, and the temperature had dropped. She stormed across the lawn and tossed the garland over the low stone wall, out of sight, onto the meadow on the other side. She turned on her heel and hurried back into the house where she bent to gather up more of the greenery that she had paid this person to unnecessarily bedeck the cottage with.

As she seized up another bough of spruce, she turned back toward the door and let out a deep gasp as she walked straight into the person standing on the front step.

"Lochlan!" she breathed, clutching her chest, still clinging onto the garland.

He chuckled at his wife as he stood before her, his cheeks flushed from the hours he had spent walking in the frosty foothills.

"What's happening here?" he asked, pushing his hair away from his forehead, damp with perspiration from the hike and from the moist winter air.

He unzipped his luminous alpinist jacket and scanned the floor by the front door, noticing the variety of fir and conifer branches at their feet.

"What's all this?"

"Oh, I - they're just some decorations," was Verity's vague response, relieved to see Lochlan home but still shaken (and mildly inebriated from the one glass of chardonnay she had speedily sunken).

"From the woods?" he asked his wife. He was chipper - the walk had clearly done him good, and he was in a jovial mood.

"Yes. Sort of. Well yes," came his wife's muddled reply.

She didn't know what to say. She didn't want to admit to him that she'd given £50 to the man he turned away yesterday. It would annoy him. He would see it as spiteful and defiant.

"I went to get some extra clippings from the forest," she lied, desperately wanting to be rid of the greenery on the cottage floor. "But it's too much. I want to throw it out."

"Why?" Lochlan asked, slinging his backpack onto the armchair by the front window and removing his frosty boots. "It's festive. It will make the cottage look even more Christmassy. Hang it up while I shower and change and we'll go into the village."

And with that, he kissed her. His mouth was bitterly cold on her own wine-tinged lips. But the kiss itself was warm and loving. He rarely issued flippant, tender kisses these days, and Verity wasn't about to start another argument with him over a bunch of conifer fronds.

While Lochlan took a shower, she spent the time begrudgingly adorning various shelves and windowsills with the greenery, twisting ivy vines around the balustrades of the staircase and placing sprigs of holly at the edges of framed paintings around the house.

By the time she had finished, Lochlan was refreshed from his shower and ready for the rest of their afternoon together. Verity was also feeling a little calmer, and more content (she'd poured herself a second glass of chardonnay) and when she stood back and assessed her decorative skills she felt happier, and admitted that the cottage was looking even more festive than before.

Her mood was lifted further when Lochlan suggested she open one of his gifts, like he had opened one of her's the evening before. The pair stood before the hearth, next to the tree, as she carefully opened a small present - a chain, with a pair of tiny silver antlers hanging from it, entwined decoratively around each other.

"I actually got it when I was in the village yesterday getting breakfast," Lochlan explained, turning her away from him and fastening it around her neck. "Thought it would be a reminder of our time here."

Verity had no doubt that their love-making on the first night at the cottage had contributed to this purchase - but she nonetheless clutched at the pendant around her neck and smiled. She turned and they kissed - a lingering kiss, before the fireplace, as if they were in a Christmas tableaux; and the unsettling incident with the pedlar at the door melted away.

✠•✠•✠

Fallows' Spinney was dark when they arrived.

It had been a grey afternoon and the thick cloud had barely let a glimmer of sunlight through since noon. By the time the Tamblyns had driven to the village and parked the car near the square, the little stone houses had their curtains drawn and fires lit inside, smoke whispering from the chimney stacks.

It was far from bustling in this sleepy hamlet. The square was bedecked with twinkling lights and festive bunting - most probably left strung up from whatever summer festivals the village threw annually, if any at all.

A few late-afternoon shoppers trotted across the square, eager to get home to their cosy firesides. Verity and Lochlan pottered, taking in the quaint wintry setting, stopping for some mulled cider at one of the three stalls on the square selling seasonal refreshments.

They walked past The Church of Abbess Eunice - the gothic-looking structure Verity had noticed from the road as they had driven past the village two nights ago. It was a ramshackle building in need of refurbishment, but grandiose in its height and architecture. The steeple ascended high and the belfry housed a fragile-looking bell, as well as a nest of birds. Jackdaws, by the sound of their catty cawing.

The few restaurants that there were in the village were mostly around the square, but Lochlan had discovered a more secluded bistro along a quieter passageway, when he had nipped in for supplies the day before. The Tamblyns walked arm-in-arm down the cobbled street, which was closed-in by the stony walls of the buildings either side of it, reaching upward toward the moody sky.

The sound of a fiddle could be heard as they walked along, and Verity could see a young man sat on a wooden stool to the side of the street. He appeared to be blind, and was playing Good King Wenceslas slowly. It was a haunting rendition, and very beautiful.

The bistro was called The Goat and was a low-ceilinged, candlelit affair with checked cloths and wicker baskets of bread on each table. The fiddler could be heard still through the thin windows, albeit less clearly. Only two other tables were occupied, as it was still only early-evening; although Verity couldn't imagine the place to ever get much busier than that.

They settled, Lochlan ordered some red wine and appetisers of French onion soup. Verity ordered a lemon sole for her entrée and Lochlan chose steak tartar with green beans.

"I thought we'd get a pheasant or a partridge for Christmas Eve," Lochlan said, taking a sip from the glass of claret he had ordered. He had ordered a bottle, tasted and poured it for the two of them.

"Sounds nice," Verity said, scratching her arm. It had been tingling a little for the past hour.

"There's that butcher on the edge of the square," Lochlan went on, gesturing vaguely towards the restaurant door. "I got our lunch from there yesterday morning when I came into town. They said they could do us a goose for Christmas Day if we fancied. Something a bit more traditional, seeing as we're in the country."

The tingling on Verity's arm had become rather more uncomfortable since coming in from the cold, and was now more of an itch.

"Verity?" Lochlan said, after she failed to reply.

"Yes?"

"Goose?"

"Yes. Goose works for me," she said, scratching with a little more vigour.

"What's wrong with your arm?" Lochlan asked, noticing her discomfort.

"It's a little itchy," she answered.

"Is it the sweater?" he offered.

"No," she said, curtly.

"Take it off, perhaps you're too warm," he suggested.

She did, stripping down to just a black strap top, revealing a red blemish on her forearm, probably not helped by her persistent scratching over the past fifteen minutes.

"Leave it alone," Lochlan instructed, pouring himself some more wine.

The fiddler had now begun playing In The Bleak Midwinter outside. The sombre tune grated on Verity as she examined the red mark.

The soups arrived, and Lochlan tucked in. Verity finished her glass of claret and poured herself another, before unenthusiastically sipping a spoonful from her own bowl of broth. She felt flushed. The heat from the soup didn't help. The rash on her arm had become increasingly irritable and it wasn't helping her mood. The candles flickering around her added to her annoyance and started contributing to a feeling of vexatious warmth.

By the time they had finished their starters (she only ate a third of her's) Verity had downed a second glass of claret. Her head was swimming a little. She was feeling impatient and fidgety.

Sat across from her, Lochlan rambled on about the hike he'd had that morning. Words were coming from his direction - words describing the rocky terrain of the foothills and about the herd of deer he had startled as dawn had broken - and she just didn't care. She wasn't listening. She began to feel increasingly annoyed with her husband.

"I got back later than I'd planned," he was saying, by this stage tucking into his steak tartar. "I'm sorry about that."

"Its fine," Verity muttered.

He looked at his wife with warmth, despite the clear consternation furrowed across her expression. He examined her lean neck and her collarbone, naked in the strap top and more prominent in the dim candlelight.

"That necklace suits you beautifully," he said, referring to the gift he'd given her that afternoon which hung between the crease at the top of her breasts.

Verity smiled. He was being overly nice. He'd had the perfect day. He had hiked, given her a gift he felt smug about and was now enjoying bloody steak and blood-red wine. Of course he was in a good mood.

"You like it don't you?" he checked.

"Of course I do. I've told you I do," she snapped.

She had clearly raised her voice, as the other tables' occupants glanced in their direction.

"Verity." He did not sound impressed.

She felt dizzy, but stood up and said: "Sorry. I'm going to use the bathroom."

Verity walked away from the table, her heels clacking noisily across the wooden bistro floor, her head swaying and her arm increasingly feeling as if it might burst into flames.

She ran it under the cold water tap once inside the restroom, which instantly soothed the pink patch that had broken out on her normally pale and flawless skin. She exhaled as she allowed the cooling sensation overtake her. She let the icy water trickle down her forearm to the tendon at her wrist, where her pulse throbbed below. She closed her eyes, trying to calm down and let her head settle.

She opened them again, after a few seconds, to come face-to-face with herself in the mirror above the basin. She looked into her own deep brown eyes, examining her reflection. She had swept her straight chestnut hair on top of her head neatly with a clip, but the sudden hot flush and her swift trot to the bathroom had caused one or two strands to come loose and fall in front of her face.

Verity felt a little transfixed by the sight of herself; not something she would usually admit to as she was a notably un-vain woman for someone so naturally attractive. But something seemed to catch her attention in this particular instance as she glared at herself in the glass.

And then she noticed it.

A strand of her hair stood out from the rest. It was one of the strands that had freed itself from the rest of her tied-up mane and fallen in front of her eyes. Still with her arm under the rush of water in the sink, Verity leaned forward toward the mirror. She allowed her eyes to focus directly on the wayward lock that flimsily danced in front of her face.

It was darker than her otherwise chocolatey mane. It was, in fact, black. She examined it as it dangled before her left eye – a streak of ebony, cutting through her otherwise tawny head of hair, swaying tauntingly away from the rest. She couldn't explain what had happened here - where this streak had come from. And, oddly, she didn't seem to care.

As the water continued to gush around her forearm, Verity realised that she had almost ceased to feel her limb at all. It felt spectacularly numb. The burning sensation had completely subsided, and in place of it was a sense of frozen anaesthesia. It felt magnificent. She swung her head backwards and allowed a euphoric moan to escape her lips.

The rest of the evening settled back into some normalcy.

Having taken the time to calm down, Verity returned to the dinner table to find Lochlan nearly finished with his steak and completely finished with the wine. Another bottle had been ordered as Verity sat back down.

She assured her husband that she was feeling much better and that it had purely been a moment of unexpected flushness. Any disgruntlement Lochlan had felt about her running off to the restroom was swiftly placated by Verity's now-amicable mood. She, in fact, felt better than she had done all evening, and was ready to continue their night out together.

She picked at her fish as the waiter delivered the second bottle of wine, and hastily accepted the offer for another glass. By this point, one of the two tables at the bistro had emptied, and the other table's patrons were sipping liquors and enjoying a coffee cake between them. The tall candles that had been burning around the restaurant had become increasingly molten and their flames dulcet, burning closer to theirs wicks, leaving The Goat shrouded in a flicker of shadow and duskiness.

Lochlan asked Verity what she had gotten up to while he had been out that morning. She told him the truth - breakfast, a walk in the garden, a nap.

She replaced the incident with the pedlar, however, with a fictitious trip to the forest to gather up some more seasonal cuttings, in order to explain the new mass of greenery Lochlan had returned to.

"You walked to the woods?" Lochlan clarified, topping up Verity's glass with the last of their second bottle of claret.

"I did," she said, seizing up the glass, raising it to say thank you and leaning back in her seat, her barely-touched lemon sole left in bitty flakes on the plate before her amid a gaggle of samphire.

"The forest up the lane, back towards Fallows' Spinney?" he asked her, weirdly inquisitive.

Verity shot him a slightly confused look, saying nothing.

Lochlan smiled and shook his head jovially. "It's just that I don't know how you got into those woods without walking all the way back towards the village," he mused. "The hedgerows that surround it are so thick and thorny. Did you really walk all that way up the lane just to get some more greenery for the house?"

He was right, she thought. That forest was dense to say the least; and realistically Verity wouldn't have bothered to schlep any further than she had to. He would have known that.

"No, not *those* woods," she corrected him, reconstructing her lie. "I went up to that copse across the moor, behind the cottage."

It was ridiculous that she was even lying in the first place about where the extra greenery had come from, and she wasn't completely sure why she was bothering to spin this silly yarn.

"Oh right. Miser's Copse, yes?" Lochlan confirmed.

"Yeah," she replied, swigging from her glass flippantly.

"I was thinking about taking a walk up that way tomorrow," Lochlan said. "What's it like?"

"I don't know. Just a bunch of trees I suppose," came Verity's slovenly reply. She was becoming increasingly drunk.

"Rocky? Would I need my climbing boots? What did you wear on your feet?" he asked.

He was such a details Nazi, and this had been what had riled Verity before she had escaped to the bathroom. This time, however, she was less wound up by her husband's pernickety questioning. Instead, she just gave into it, and fleshed out her fictional trip to the copse further, with extra facts and details. The wine helped immensely with this.

"It wasn't too rocky," she said, making it up as she spoke. "I wore my boots. The ones I don't care about. Didn't take too long to cross that field to the top of the hill where the trees are.

"When you get up there, you have to walk around the outskirts of the copse before you come to a break in the pine trees on the east edge of it. There's a path that takes you through the trees and there's this stone in the ground. It's a bit like a gravestone and it's got Miser's Copse carved into it."

Lochlan listened intently as his wife continued to reel off her completely fabricated description of the copse.

"You go along the path. It's pretty dense in there, and actually goes a lot deeper than you'd expect looking at it from the cottage. I took some clippings from the low-hanging trees at the edge of the path, and walked in further enough to get to the middle of the copse, where there is a clearing. A couple of sheep had actually wandered into it, I guess from the moor, and they scattered off; I think I must have frightened them. They must often go into the copse, there were bits of wool caught on lots of the undergrowth around the clearing. God knows how they manage to get in if they don't use the pathway. Maybe they do, I suppose.

"Not much else to say about it; I kept to the path and the

clearing, I suppose if you hiked through the wilder parts of the copse it would be more of a challenge, which I know is what you like."

Lochlan nodded, sipping the last of his wine, the dancing candle in the centre of their table flickering across his gaze.

"I couldn't see much beyond the path, it's pretty dark in there. Quite rough - a lot of stones and ferns and nettles. The ground looked quite wild and untouched. The soil was pretty dried up and loose. Actually, there was - "

Verity stopped speaking. She couldn't carry on, and didn't want to say any more. She couldn't comprehend what she had just been saying. It didn't make sense to her. It was like a stream of consciousness had poured from her mouth, without any reason to it at all.

She had reeled off a description of a place she had never been, almost as if she *had* been there. And why? What had been the point in doing that? Lochlan, with all his intricacies and specifics, was used to Verity's vagueness when it came to the finer details of things. She could have said, "I went in, walked around, came out, went home," and he wouldn't have given it a second thought. Why had she felt the need to spill out such a descriptive tale about that bunch of trees on the hill?

What's more, he had expressly stated that he planned to visit it himself tomorrow. Why had she painted such a picture that surely wasn't accurate? He would see for himself that she had made the whole thing up.

Except, she hadn't.

She couldn't grasp how or why, but she was more than certain that the way she had described Miser's Copse was precisely how it actually looked. From the stone sign on the path, to the sheep wool in the thorns, to what she knew was hidden in the undergrowth amongst the loose earth beyond the clearing.

It had been this that had forced her to stop mid-sentence. What she had been about to mention was not something she wanted to include in her overly-specific vignette of the copse.

"What?" Lochlan said, noticing that she had abruptly stopped speaking.

Verity realised that she must have been wearing a look of concern on her face; concern over what she was saying, why she was saying it and how she was *able* to say it. She had never been to Miser's Copse - this made no logical sense.

She swiftly shot her eyes up to meet her husband's as he smiled gently at her from across the table. The bistro had now emptied, save for the two of them and the staff who were loitering around the kitchen door. She had barely realised that the other couple had finished, paid and left. The sound of the fiddler outside still persisted, but Verity only realised it in that moment, somehow managing to block out all surrounding distractions as she had spoken about the copse.

"There was what?" Lochlan asked, entreating her to finish her description.

Enough of this, she thought.

She glanced down at Lochlan's empty wine glass, his hand resting on the base of it. She shrugged and looked back at his face. She smiled at her husband, reaching across the table and touching his hand, stroking it sensually.

"I've lost my train of thought," she said. "Anyway, why don't we order a couple of brandies and get out of here."

With this, Verity slipped one foot out of its high heel and across the floor under the table towards Lochlan, gently caressing his leg with it. She was being positively brazen. Yes, they were a married couple, but Verity had been afraid to make such advances on her husband since everything had happened over the last year. This was either progress, or a stupidly bold move.

But Lochlan welcomed it.

"Let's get a bottle to go, shall we?" he whispered, his cheeks flush from the warmth of the bobbing flame between them, from the red wine he had consumed and from the sensation of his wife fondling his ankle with her naked toes.

Verity leant back as Lochlan waved at the waiter to come back over. She looked at her husband in the low-light of the bistro, his dark features striking, the sound of The Holly And The

Ivy creeping through the windows from the fiddle in the cobbled street outside. She felt a desire for him that she hadn't felt for a long while. She grinned at him and pushed back the jet black strands that fell across her face.

There were now two of them.

᛭᛭᛭

That evening, Verity and Lochlan made love again.

They had left the car in the village and taken a cab (probably the only one in Fallows' Spinney) back to The Spinney House, where they had sat in the back seat and sneakily sipped from the bottle of brandy they had bought from The Goat. They had sat close together, his arm around her shoulders, her fingers sensually running up and down his thigh.

On arrival at the cottage gates, Lochlan had overpaid the driver with what looked like two £20 notes and had helped his wife out of the car, walking her to the front door of the house like a gentleman. He fumbled with the key in the lock, putting the side-door key in first before laughing and switching it for the right one.

As he did, Verity waited on the step behind him, hugging her coat around her body. The Christmas air was bitterly cold, especially out in the open of the countryside. It drifted in, damply, from the moors that encircled the walled garden.

Verity rested her gaze on the cottage door and noticed the Christmas wreath fixed to it, made by the pedlar.

Without thinking, she leant across her husband who was hunched over the door handle attempting to unlock it in his brandy and wine-infused state, reached for the wreath and snatched it as calmly as she could from the nail it hung from.

She tossed it to her left, watching it disappear into the camellia bushes that lined the front of the house. As she did, Lochlan unlocked the door and opened it for his wife, who laughed lazily and strutted inside in front of him, the brandy bottle under her arm.

Had he noticed the wreath, he would have known Verity had lied to him. He would have guessed the pedlar had been back at their doorstep. And she wanted nothing to sully their evening.

Inside, they lit the fire and turned on the Christmas lights. Lochlan fetched glasses from the kitchen and they drank more liquor in front of the hearth, the boughs of bay and spruce lining the mantle above them, encircling them with earthy seasonal scents. The glass ornaments on the Christmas tree cast colourful reflections across the living room as the couple enjoyed their sweet brandy, both of their heads swimming delightfully.

Lochlan kissed his wife. She tasted the alcohol on his breath. Her lips became cloven to his, both sets sickly and candied from the liquor. She inhaled her husband. He radiated an effervescent warmth, all of the time. It was something to do with his staunch manliness - he was always intoxicatingly clement. It aroused her. And, in spite of her husband's physical magnetism not changing over their troubled year, she had not desired him this powerfully for a long time.

Not ever, perhaps.

The feeling was evidently mutual. Lochlan's kiss was firm and assertive as his own lips pressed hard against Verity's. He pushed his weight into her. She felt a blazing heat radiate from both Lochlan and the fire that had gained momentum in the hearth next to them. He opened his mouth, widely; his sweet, wet tongue sliding from between his teeth into Verity's mouth. It expertly slithered, sensually seeking out her own tongue, finding it, locking onto it. She widened her mouth and allowed him to penetrate it as deeply as he wished. She had not experienced such intimacy in a long while, even on their first night at the cottage; and every breath he took as he kissed her exhumed the bitterness that she still felt for him beneath the surface. She was open, at last, to truly receiving him again. And she didn't care how it happened.

Lochlan undressed his wife slowly, first pulling her sweater over her head, then her strap top, letting it flutter to the floor. He unzipped her skin-tight jeans, sliding them down her thighs.

He planted a gentle kiss on each thigh as he knelt before her. Her skin was feeling almost unnaturally hot - from Lochlan, from the fire, from the passion she felt for her husband. He removed her jeans entirely, leaving her merely clad in a black bra and matching underwear, and kissed her skin as he travelled back up her torso, raising from his position on his knees.

His lips met her's once again and pressed against them. She reached for the buttons of his shirt and fumbled with them, unclasping them one at a time. He moved his strong hands into her hair as she removed his shirt and cradled her head, his tongue once again thrusting into her throat. He unclipped her hair as she unzipped his slacks, feeling the firmness that had sprung beneath them. Her chestnut mane fell loosely about her shoulders, which were now balmy with a hotness that both disturbed and excited her.

With force, Lochlan spun Verity around, facing away from him. She felt him behind her, his hard penis pressing against her underwear, dampening them slightly from his excitement. He brushed her brunette tresses away from her shoulders, leaving her neck exposed. She closed her eyes with anticipation as he began to kiss her neck. It felt as if it was throbbing; the veins in her throat almost ready to burst.

She slowly opened her eyes again and peered directly forward, at the living room window. It was pitch black outside, nothing out there save for the vast sweeping meadows. Her reflection stared back at her, crystal clear in the large blank glass pane. Although only faint, she made out marks on her neck and the top of her chest, above her breasts. A red, flushed mark - similar to that on her arm. It travelled from the tops of her breasts, up her chest, to her collarbone, snaking upwards.

Lochlan's grip on her from behind became firmer. She breathed, loudly and with depth. He pressed himself harder into her, his groin, still entombed in his slacks, clearly desperate to be freed. She stared forward as he did so, scrutinising the rash on her neck which felt almost searing and sharp. From behind, Lochlan licked her, his sodden, brandy-tinged tongue slathering her shoulders.

She gasped, pleasurably, her two solitary black strands of hair falling forward over her eyes, which she closed once more.

She felt Lochlan unclip her bra, letting it fall off her body, before he knelt once again, bringing her underwear down as he did so. She felt him part her thighs. He kissed them once again. He licked them. The licking became sucking. He was sucking at the skin between her legs. It was odd and unfamiliar and excitingly vampiric.

This went on for what felt like several long, enticing minutes, with Lochlan slowly inserting his tongue between Verity's thighs, eventually moving it inside her. She moved forward, bringing him with her on his knees, to support herself on the armchair that sat in the corner, in front of the window. She positioned herself in the chair, kneeling on it, opening her legs so that Lochlan could continue to work his tongue inside her. She leant her naked body forward, pushing her weight onto the back of the armchair. Her face was now staring back at itself in the window glass. She locked her eyes onto her own gaze as she enjoyed the sensation of her husband tasting her. She pushed back into his face so that he would feel the full force of her enjoyment. She gripped onto the back of the chair, squelching the cushioned headrest in her palms.

She was uncomfortably hot, but she didn't care; and as Lochlan stood up behind her and entered her from behind, she found herself suddenly transfixed on his reflection in the window pane. The firelight flickered in the backdrop in the hearth, Lochlan's tall torso a powerful silhouette in the foreground, masterfully taking her.

She wondered whether or not she had ever been this aroused. She leant further forward and pressed her forehead against the coolness of the window pane, the silver chain Lochlan had gifted her swinging from around her neck, the tiny antlers clinking at the glass. She breathed rhythmically as he thrusted into her. She imagined his buttocks clenching sternly with every deep movement. It aroused her even more greatly than before.

The pulsating feeling in her neck now reverberated around her entire frame, the heat prickling her with its intensity.

She suddenly became very aware of the room; and the earthy intricacies that decorated it. Just in that moment, it was as if the boughs of pine and sprigs of juniper that had been brought in from the wintry landscape surrounding the cottage had sprung to life, as Lochlan deeply penetrated her, a gruff moan escaping him every now and then.

It was as if her body, which was coursing with this mixture of heat and desire, was in league with the room. It was dizzying and, for a moment, felt oppressive. She felt as if the pine garlands and ivy vines were creeping from the banister and the mantle, suddenly fixated on Verity. It was as if they were coming for her, ready to enwrap her, like a clan of boa constrictors, honing in on her in her state of fervid submission.

The thought of it was too much for Verity; yet she did not want Lochlan to stop. She pressed her forehead more firmly into the window, then turned her head slightly and allowed her cheek to rest on the glass. It was cooling and soothing. Every part of her body was moist apart from her mouth. It was suddenly horrifically dry. Barren.

While Lochlan continued to thrust into her, Verity opened her mouth, unleashed her tongue, and licked the glass. She sucked on the moisture of the window - a sheer barrier between the intensity of the sweltering living room and the freezing wintry moors outside. She closed her eyes as she rolled her tongue along the pane, her breath fogging up the glass as she did so. It worked; it satisfied her. It quenched her.

She pulled her head back from the window and found herself lilting her body in time with Lochlan's thrusts, each of them breathing harshly as the sex drew closer to its finale.

She felt incredibly focused, suddenly. She rested her eyes on her own in the reflection of the glass. She stared sternly at herself. She watched her face, flushed and sweaty. She could feel herself close to climax. Her heart thrashed inside her chest.

She locked her eyes on her visage. And then, beyond: into the darkness outside. Verity could not see anything but the black-ness of the frosty, winter's night - but she knew it was out there. Something was watching her. A presence, joining her and Loch-lan, glaring in at them, burning through them.

It was unpleasant and intrusive and violating. It hated her. It was repulsed, yet also intrigued. Jealous, yet elated. It was mal-eficent and bestial and embittered. It unsettled her yet excited her at the same time.

She screamed, her forehead pressed against the glass, her eyes still staring, widely, erratically, outside at deep, deadening blackness, as Lochlan brought her into a state of euphoria she had never felt, ever, before.

DECEMBER 23RD.

They had never had a night like that.

Verity replayed it in her mind as she lay in bed and stared at the low, whitewashed bedroom ceiling the following morning.

She felt warm; the bedroom was almost muggy. It could have been a balmy summer's morning the way she lay sprawled out on the crisp white linen of the bed, the duvet tossed to the floor, only part of her naked body covered with one of the sheets. Lochlan lay entwined in another sheet, also naked. His lean frame lay motionless, save for his chest as it moved up and down with every deep breath he made as he slept.

They had disappeared to bed in the early hours of the morning with the rest of the brandy bottle, which now lay strewn across the other side of the bedroom on the floor. They had started to lose themselves in another gust of passion as they had gotten to the bedroom, but their intoxicated state had ended in a fit of giggles.

They had then simply laid next to one another, breathless, before falling asleep.

Verity turned in the bed slowly, so as not to wake her husband, who was notoriously a light sleeper. She watched him as he lay on his back, his head tilted back, his lips closed, a gentle consistent inhale-exhale coming from him. His forehead was furrowed a little, a frown on his face. His typically hardened expression remained, even when he slept - when one is supposed to appear at their most serene.

Staring at him, Verity realised she hadn't noticed this about Lochlan before - how stern he still looked, in sleep. But she also couldn't recall the last time she had watched him sleeping like this; if ever at all.

Her eyes travelled down his neck, to his strong shoulder-blades, along to the top of his arm. It looked a little blotchy, and sore. She tried to recall any specific moments of passion from the night before where she had grabbed him a little too hard. She couldn't think.

Then it dawned on her: the mark on Lochlan resembled her own uncomfortable skin irritation that had flared up at The Goat. At this, she glanced down at her forearm. The rash was still there - in fact, it looked a little redder. She could feel that it was still evident on her breasts and chest and neck, too. The hot air in the stuffy bedroom would not have helped in cooling them down, she thought. The room had an east-facing window and the morning sunlight was streaming in through the glass.

She glanced back at her husband's bicep, examining his ver-sion of the same mark that she had. It looked sore. She reached over to her bedside table and picked up the tub of hand lotion that sat on it, next to the cluster of jewellery she had drunkenly managed to remove and dump there. Quietly she unscrewed the lid, took some onto her finger and gently massaged it into Loch-lan's muscle, hoping to soothe it.

He didn't wake; he didn't even stir. He just slept.

She put some on her own arm and chest for good meas-ure, shrugged off the mystery of their matching marks, and stepped slowly from the bed, reaching for the nightgown that had remained untouched on the chair in the corner all night. She slipped it over her head and tip-toed across the bedroom, desperate to get out of the claustrophobic heat and downstairs into the cooler kitchen.

As she did, Verity accidentally kicked the empty brandy bot-tle across the floor, into the skirting board at the foot of the wall by the door.

It caused a "clink" as it hit the wood.

She turned slowly to see that Lochlan hadn't moved. This man would wake if an owl so much as hooted outside the window at their home in the city. But he lay still, quiet, sleeping.

Odd, Verity thought, as she slipped out of the room.

It was a wonder the cottage hadn't burnt down in the night. Verity arrived downstairs to be reminded that they had lit candles and the fire, none of which they had extinguished before disappearing to the bedroom.

Items of their clothing lay here and there, and the floor before the hearth had a throw rug and pillows placed on it, where they had sat and made their way through the brandy, gradually becoming more and more amorous. The rug was horrifyingly close to the fireplace and one cushion had been tossed onto the basket of logs by the grate. The cushion teetered on the edge of a chunk of silver birch, thankfully remaining there and not toppling onto the glowing coals. The flames in the fireplace had died, leaving crackling embers among the blackened wood, a trickle of smoke slowly snaking upwards, disappearing into the chimney. The candles had all burnt down to their wicks. Runny wax - thankfully hardened by now - had dripped down each candles' yellow torso, dangerously gaining on the wooden surfaces they were dotted around.

Verity gritted her teeth at their carelessness, relieved that their fit of passion hadn't led to a catastrophe. She then walked barefoot across the living room and into the kitchen to make some coffee.

The mahogany floors were cooler in there, and the frosted window panes proved it was another bitterly cold day outside. Yet, Verity was still feeling warm, and was glad of the chilly boards on her bare feet.

As the percolator churned out the coffee she so desperately needed to wake up, Verity thought about the evening she had had. It had started gratingly - but ended ecstatically. She felt good; she felt liberated.

Standing in the kitchen of The Spinney House, the day before Christmas Eve, in her lacy nightdress, bare foot, she thought of her strong, sensual husband still asleep amid the sheets. The sheets they had sat naked in while they sipped brandy into their mouths and kissed each other, letting the warm sickly liquid trickle down their chins and onto the crisp, clean linens, staining them.

Thinking about it made her feel marvellous.

Verity stepped away from the counter and into the centre of the kitchen, where the sunlight hit the deep dark wood of the cool floor. Her feet still cold on the mahogany, the percolator still dribbling its deep roast into the coffee pot, filling the room with a rich, bitter aroma, Verity slipped the straps of her nightdress from her shoulders. She let the garment slide from her smooth body down to her feet. She stood naked, basking in the sunlight from the kitchen window, her head back, her eyes closed. She allowed the warmth from the wintry sun, the cool from the wooden floors, and the scent from the brewing coffee encircle her naked body. She felt wonderful.

She spun slowly, and then again. She stopped facing the window, bathed in white light from the frosty sunshine. She let the warm rays blind her closed eyes, before slowly opening them once more.

As she did, a contented smile on her lips, Verity saw a black shadow stood before her, at the window.

Dazzled by the light, she squinted at the shape, unsure of what it was. As she focused, Verity made out the outline of a figure. It was outside the window, looking in.

At her.

This sudden realisation forced the smile to drop from Verity's face, and she moved one hand up above her eyes in an attempt to see into the stream of light that was blinding her. She blinked and tried to focus, gradually realising it was a man.

He was small. He was peering in - staring straight at her. His face was twisted into a smile, his cracked lips a little parted to reveal one dirty, sharp-looking tooth.

It was him - the man from yesterday. The man who had come to the door. The pedlar. He was looking in at Verity's naked body, hunched over in the way he had been the day before as he'd stood on the front steps of the cottage.

Verity felt disorientated. The bright sun, her nakedness, and the man she had been trying to forget about standing before her, having appeared as if from nowhere, unsettled her. The coffee machine made it's shrill, piercing noise to signify it had finished brewing, startling her further. Verity glanced at it before quickly bending to seize up her nightdress and hold it up to cover herself.

The percolator screamed at her from across the kitchen, but she looked quickly at the window once more.

No-one was there.

᛭ᛁ᛭ᛁ᛭

The strangest thing about seeing the man at the window was that Verity hadn't felt frightened like she had during her encounter with him the day before. She had felt startled, but not afraid; and she couldn't fathom why this was.

This peculiar (and rather eerie) man had returned to their house after practically vanishing from thin air the afternoon before and had watched her from the window during a very uninhibited and vulnerable moment. Or rather - moments; for Verity was sure, on reflection, that he had been watching her and Lochlan make love the night before through the window in the living room. She had felt someone outside at the time, shrouded by the frozen night; yet her euphoria had muddied her ability to care.

Now, the morning after, she cared.

The same man had also uttered words to Verity that had chilled her to her core the last time she had seen him. Words that were still lingering.

You killed her.

Yet Verity was feeling less unsettled as she sat, nightdress back on, at the kitchen table with her cup of coffee, one eye still on the window. The old man was on her mind, but her feelings about him were confused. It was as if she couldn't decide how to react to his reappearance.

Regardless, she didn't have time to contemplate it, as Lochlan soon appeared at the kitchen door wearing just his boxer briefs. He was on the hunt for some of the freshly-brewed coffee that had filled the cottage with its aroma. Thirsty from their night before, he was like a blood hound that had caught the scent of a doe.

She didn't tell him what had happened. She didn't want to. He poured coffee, kissed her forehead and sat across from her at the table, tucking into fresh fruit ravenously that he had extracted from the fridge.

He was in a good mood: he had enjoyed a night of steak, brandy and sex. But there was something different about Lochlan, besides his new chipper demeanour.

Verity nursed her coffee as she watched him bite devilishly into a wedge of grapefruit, the acidic red juice dripping down his chin as he did so. His face was warm - almost boyish and gleeful. He licked his lips before reaching for his coffee, which he gulped, black and bitter, taking an uncouth chug from it before continuing to wolf down the raw fruit.

Then Verity realised it. She saw what was different about him. Lochlan's dark blonde hair had a streak through it. A deep black streak, just like the ones she had found on her own head.

He dropped the grapefruit rind onto the plate in front of him and reached once more for his coffee. Noticing his wife staring at him, he paused.

"What?" he asked, an inquisitive smile on his lips, wet with grapefruit flesh.

"Nothing," Verity replied, smiling back, subconsciously brushing her own black strands of hair back behind her ear as she did so.

Lochlan raised himself out of his chair and lent across the table to kiss Verity, a sour citric taste on his lips.

She inhaled his scent. He was warm, notes of aftershave still evident on his skin from their evening out. His torso radiated a scent of dry sweat and heady brandy. As he pulled away from her, she watched his body - taut and toned. Her eyes travelled down his strong chest, his stomach, his abdomen contracting enticingly as he moved. She gazed at the outline of his genitals underneath his white briefs, and admired the tops of his strong thighs.

She desired him. She had desired him the night before, and she wanted him again now. Her explicit thoughts and his tender kiss proved their animosity had waned greatly overnight.

"What's on the agenda for today?" he asked her, sinking back down in his seat and taking another gulp from his mug. "Are we going to walk up to those trees on the hill? It sounds nice up there."

"Oh. Sure," she said, thoughts of sex leaving her, remembering the elaborate tale she had spontaneously spun about Miser's Copse at dinner.

"What's it like out?" Lochlan asked, peering past Verity toward the window the hunched old man had been at just ten minutes ago.

"Seems nice."

With that, Lochlan stood and headed out of the kitchen, back into the living room and to the front door. Verity remained sat at the table as she heard her husband open it with a slight creak and disappear onto the steps outside.

There was silence for a moment - apart from the odd chirp from a robin coming from the front garden. A rush of chilly air blew into the kitchen sending a shudder through Verity, still in nothing but her flimsy nightie.

After a minute, Lochlan called in from outside: "Verity?"

"Yes?"

Another pause; after which she heard Lochlan re-enter the house and shut the door behind him. He appeared back at the kitchen entrance holding a wreath - the one she had drunkenly ripped down and tossed into the undergrowth when they had arrived home the night before.

"What's this? I found it in the bushes," he enquired, dangling the delicately woven circle of seasonal leaves from one of his fingers.

It had had better days, having been swiped off the door by Verity, chucked into the shrubs and left in the damp frosty earth all night.

"A wreath," she said, unsure of what else to say.

"Where's it from?" Lochlan asked.

"You found it in the bushes?" she enquired, ambiguously dodging the question.

"Yeah. Well, it was sticking out from the flower bed, that's why it caught my attention. Looked like it had been dumped there."

"Must have blown off in the wind," she offered.

"From where?"

"The door, I suppose."

"There wasn't a wreath on the door, was there?"

Verity just shrugged. This was ridiculous, she thought.

So she confessed: "I bought it off that old man. He came back while you were out yesterday. Actually, he gave it to me as a gift. So I bought a couple of other bits from him, to decorate with."

Lochlan looked irritated. "He came back?"

"Yes," Verity replied simply.

Lochlan tutted. "That cheeky bugger. I already told him we didn't want any of that junk. How much did you spend?"

This annoyed Verity. She stood up and faced her husband.

"Does it matter? If you'd been less uptight about buying something from him in the first place I wouldn't have felt so bad for him," she argued, and then remembered seeing him pay the cab driver the night before. "Anyway, you lied about not having any cash. You had plenty. You paid for the taxi home last night, I saw you."

Lochlan rolled his eyes at his wife.

"I didn't want any of that crap. I still don't," he said, tossing the dishevelled wreath onto the kitchen table, bits of sodden moss flaking from it as it landed.

"Well it's my money," Verity said, already losing interest in the argument. "I'll spend it on what I want."

"And I won't spend mine on what I *don't* want!" Lochlan snapped back, stopping to clearly contemplate whether or not what he had said actually made any sense.

A smirk slithered across Verity's indignant pout. Lochlan attempted to stifle his own sudden smile.

"You really wanted all those branches and twigs and bits of tree clogging up that living room?" he asked her, flinging one arm in the direction of the lounge. "It's like the Temperate House at Kew in there."

"Yes. I did," Verity lied, the "I did" coming out as a giggle.

Lochlan's frown cracked and his naked shoulders began to shake.

They both burst into wicked laughter.

╬╬╬

Having showered and dressed, Verity and Lochlan left The Spinney House wrapped up in their thick jackets and scarves. Lochlan wore his hiking boots, while Verity put on the shoes she had told him she'd worn yesterday on her fictitious jaunt across the moor to Miser's Copse.

Locking the now wreath-less front door behind them (Lochlan had thrown it in the bin, unsalvageable from its night in the undergrowth) they headed away from the cottage and along the lane, to the stile that led into the meadow.

Verity's boots squelched in the boggy earth as Lochlan helped her over the stile and down onto the grass. It had been a frosty night and a low mist still lay wispily across the field, ensuring the earth was adequately quaggy underfoot. Verity linked her arm around her husband's as they hiked briskly across the fen. It was a clear day, which meant it was colder. The sun was now loitering behind a haze of cloud, adding to the chill. The marshy field stretched out before them, dotted here

58

and there with rocks and sheep, clumps of bulrushes sprouting intermittently from the mist that clung to the ground.

As the landscape rose gradually into a hill, Miser's Copse stood on the horizon, pullulating from the fret-like grey that smothered the grass. The trees looked dark against the white sky above, the eclectic mix of pine and hawthorn clumped closely together, interrupted here and there by the barren, blackened trunks of long-dead trees.

Verity thought again about how she had described the copse to her husband; the oddly-detailed way she had listed precisely how one gets into it and what one will find once amongst the trees. It didn't matter now whether it was or wasn't as she had described it; Lochlan knew that the greenery hadn't been hand-picked by his wife, and that she had bought it from the pedlar instead. This, however, did nothing to settle her when they reached the edge of the pine trees to the east of the copse to discover a break in the bushes, turning into a pathway through the shrubs - just as she had described it.

"Here we are," Lochlan said, leading the way into the copse.

Verity glanced behind her, down the hill towards The Spinney House, the road and the forest that separated them from Fallows' Spinney in the distance. She wasn't afraid; yet, she felt a strange desire to drink in her surroundings once more, as if she would maybe never come out of Miser's Copse again.

There was an unsettled feeling in the pit of Verity's stomach. It had suddenly developed as they had reached the trees. A tingling inside her body had come on as she had noticed the pathway, right where she said it was going to be. It was a conflicting recipe of apprehension and excitement.

Lochlan had already vanished beyond the pines. She followed, stepping through the chink in the undergrowth, finding herself under the canopy of evergreen boughs that hung above their heads.

And she knew what she would see next.

It's a bit like a gravestone, and it's got Miser's Copse carved into it.

She thought about the detailed account she had given the

night before, as Lochlan had listened, swirling his claret around in its bulbous glass. And there it was: the stone. It was tomb-like in appearance and protruded from the crusted earth, the words "Miser's Copse" etched into it. Just as she had told him. It was damp and dotted with lichen. The thorny brambles that poked out of the trees behind the stone reached for it, like the tentacles of an octopus rising from the blue, clutching to claim the tomb for its own.

Lochlan hadn't stopped to assess the cracked slab of rock. Instead, he was marching along the pebbly path, strewn with spindly frost-tipped twigs and flaky leaves left over from the autumn. The pines on either side of the path were thick. The track led through them, the lower branches enveloping Lochlan as he continued to walk further into the copse, his slender figure disappearing amid the blue spruce.

Verity gave the "Miser's Copse" stone another glance and hurried to catch up to him. He was clearly in one of his no-nonsense moods where, rather than actually enjoy a leisurely walk together in the countryside on the day before Christmas Eve, it was a military hike. There was no time for dithering when Lochlan was feeling adventurous. He wanted to investigate the copse that had been looming ominously over their cottage from the top of the hill since they had arrived. He wanted to get amongst it, see it for himself, get out, and tick this particular To Do off his list.

Verity jogged lightly along the path and caught up with her husband. He heard her behind him and, without turning, reached back and offered his hand. She took it, welcoming someone to hold onto as they headed into what was a deceptively thick gathering of trees. It was more of a micro-forest, Verity thought to herself, as the wide branches of pine slapped against their windbreakers, their tread a little unsteady on the rock-ribbed pathway.

It had become quite dark. Verity peered upwards as she allowed Lochlan to lead her along, trusting he knew where to go. The conifers stretched tall above them and leant into each other the higher they got, creating a vaulted canopy above the path that only allowed a few slight patches of the white sky through.

Lochlan made a pained sound all of a sudden, briskly letting go of his wife's hand and stopping still.

"What?" Verity asked him.

He turned to her, his right arm held up. He had been wearing his jacket sleeves rolled up and there was a thick, nasty cut running along his forearm. It was oozing fresh blood, trickling down his skin, like a streak of lightening across a dark ambit.

"Oh, what happened?" Verity said, unhelpfully.

She was hardly concerned for her husband. He had once trodden on a scorpion in the Australian outback, presumed it wasn't poisonous and carried on his bush hike. Verity hadn't known him when this happened. Lochlan's mother had told her about it when she had met his parents for the first time at a pub lunch in Wiltshire. It was known among the Tamblyn family as "The Australia Incident". She had warned Verity that Lochlan was a flippant man's man who would give her a lifetime of worry if they ever got married.

"Caught it on a thorn or something," Lochlan said, dabbing the cut with his other hand, smearing some of the blood unhelpfully along his arm.

Verity looked to the side of the pathway and noticed a wayward briar, snaking from the thick spruce that lined the track. It looked black and jagged, its thorns protruding like porcupine quills in every direction. The branches enveloping the narrow path swayed lightly and created a rustling above. The sound sent an icy shot through Verity. She watched the outstretched bramble, swaying along with the spruce fronds. It appeared to slither back into the foliage, as if it were a retreating adder, biting a passer-by and recoiling into the gorse.

"Meh. It'll dry. Come On," Lochlan said, keen to get going again, as if Verity had been the one to stop in the first place.

The pathway began to widen a little and the trunks of the trees seemed to disperse further back. Low-growing hawthorn bushes started to sprout up to line the path instead. They were tangled and dense. Verity noticed flossy-looking clumps dotted here and there – white wisps hanging like tiny ghosts from the mess of brambles.

Sheep.

They must often go into the copse, there were bits of wool caught on lots of the undergrowth around the clearing.

Another of the details Verity had recounted the night before seemed to be materialising, inexplicably.

God knows how they manage to get in if they don't use the pathway. Maybe they do, I suppose.

Even this had been a premonition of sorts, finding herself wondering the same thing now; but thoughts of roving sheep were soon gone, as Verity was faced with yet another chapter in her pre-destined tale of the copse.

The pathway widened further, the bushes thinned out and they found themselves in a clearing. It was *the* clearing; the very one she had described. It was gloomy and the trees seemed to be at their highest in this part of the copse, towering up to completely block out the sky. It was the height of winter and very few leaves were on the branches above. Yet, somehow, it was dark. The boughs above - pine, oak, horse-chestnut and various unknown dead branches, blackened and jagged - seemed to wind upwards to meet in an archway overhead, creating a peak. A summit. It was as if they were inside a circus tent - a gloomy, macabre, scraggy circus tent, made up of vein-like branches.

This was the heart of the copse, Verity decided.

Lochlan stood with his hands on his hips in the centre of the clearing, looking around. His arm had already started to dry, but streaks of red had travelled along it, like tiny estuaries of blood.

"Where'd you get all that holly then? I can't see any holly trees in here."

He was looking around the clearing. Verity watched him, unsure of what he was getting at. She stared back at him, confused.

He then tore his eyes away from the surroundings and looked

at her, an expression of realisation now developing on his face.

"Oh. Hang on," he said slowly. "You bought all that stuff to decorate the house from that old boy at the door."

It wasn't a question, he was thinking out loud. Yet Verity nodded anyway, understanding.

"So you didn't come up here yesterday like you told me you had," he finished.

Verity had presumed he had figured this out that morning in the kitchen, when she had admitted to buying the holly and ivy from the old man's cart. She thought he - a clever man - had worked out that her story about walking to the copse the day before was just a cover up. They hadn't talked about this - she had just presumed. Yet it was clear now that Lochlan was only just putting two and two together. And as he did, he looked slightly alarmed.

"If you've never been into this copse before - how did you know it looked like this?" he asked, slowly.

Verity shifted her weight from one foot to the other, tossing her hair back out of her face.

"Yeah - it's weird isn't it?" she said with a shrug and a thin smile.

Lochlan appeared to be amused.

"You're clairvoyant," he said, a playful grin on his face. "You're a witch."

He was joking around, yet the word seemed to reverberate around the clearing.

Witch.

"Shut up," Verity laughed back, putting her hands to her face in mock-coyness.

The couple that had arrived in Fallows' Spinney just three days ago weren't the straight-laced, awkward, damaged pair they had been back in London. They had become rather playful. In the last 24 hours, they had changed.

"Witch!" Lochlan said again, holding out his blood-streaked arm and pointing at his wife. "You're the witch of Miser's Copse!"

"Shut *up!*" Verity said again, this time picking up a harmless pebble and tossing it in Lochlan's direction. "You really are an idiot!"

But then she stopped. The smile faded from her lips as she remembered. She remembered what she had started to tell Lochlan over the flickering candlelight of The Goat the night before. She remembered what she had been about to say, and why she had stopped herself saying it. And having changed the subject over their dinner, she hadn't thought about it again.

Until now.

Now that she was stood in the very spot she had fabricated just hours ago, she recalled the detail she had left out. She turned and looked behind her, at the thick trees that lined the clearing. They looked dark and unwelcoming. And she knew why. She knew what was just a few feet from them, hidden amid the undergrowth.

"Verity?" Lochlan spoke, an inquisitive lilt in his voice.

She was engrossed in the trees. She stared at them with wonder. She knew what was hidden in them. She knew it was unpleasant and macabre. Yet she wanted to go and see it. She wanted to show her husband.

Verity turned and smiled airily at Lochlan. "Want to go off piste?" she asked, playful again.

He smiled back, not really comprehending; so she reached for his hand - the bloodstained one - and pulled him along with her as she marched into the dense trees.

It was now a role-reversal: Verity was now leading the way, dragging Lochlan along behind her, through a much denser, much rougher part of the copse. There was no path, they were very much off the beaten track. The ground was stony and the earth was hard and frozen. Barely a shard of daylight could make its way through the branches above, charred and rotten, mostly dead in this part of the little thicket.

This time, Verity was in charge of where they were going; but Lochlan didn't appear to mind. She guessed that he was enjoying seeing this adventurous side of his wife, and that he was glad to be roughing it in the wilds of the undergrowth.

A little further, Verity calculated, walking briskly through the trees. A little further.

"Here." She came to a halt, Lochlan stopping beside her. "Look at that."

Verity pointed at the ground in front of them. Her outstretched finger trembled a little - from excitement, from nerves, from fear? She didn't really know.

"Jesus!" Lochlan squinted and took a step forward, looking at the earth before them.

It was a shallow grave.

The rocky plot was fashioned in a distinct oblong shape, between two gnarled, dead tree trunks. It was looser than the rest of the forest floor. It was a crumbly mass of soil. The earth was sporadic, heaped in places, sparse in parts. It looked recently tampered with, yet ancient at the same time. At the head of it protruding from the mud was a jagged piece of wood, spindly and tilting slightly. It had another twig-like piece hammered across it with a rust-encrusted nail, forming a cross shape. And hanging from it was a fresh Christmas wreath. It was stunningly made - blue pine, dotted about with cuttings of elderberry and mistletoe. It made Verity smile, despite the highly macabre setting they found themselves standing in. There was something incredibly sad and eldritch about the tableaux in front of them, in the deepest, most hidden corner of Miser's Copse.

The grave looked as if it had been visited recently, the wreath so fresh that it sparkled with dew drops in the few streaks of light that managed to slither through the trees. The grave looked like it had only recently been dug. The shallowness of it and the messiness of the mound of earth looked as if someone had been digging (or filling in) this tomb and had left the job unfinished.

Yet the twiggy cross was very final. And the wreath adorning it was ceremonial and decorative.

The wreath.

It was hand-crafted in a manner that immediately reminded Verity of the one she had been gifted by the pedlar. It was of the same fashion - delicate, thoughtfully-made and striking. Verity felt a sudden sadness that hers had ended up in the mud and consequently disposed of, like garbage.

The graveside wreath also looked like the one that Verity had noticed hanging from the sign on the road to Miser's Copse when they had arrived in Fallows' Spinney three days before - presumably also made by the pedlar. Had the old man put this wreath here, too, Verity wondered? Had that decrepit soul been out here to the most dense and unruly part of the copse to place this wreath on this grave?

Lochlan shifted, startling her a little, and walked over to the head of the grave, careful not to tread on any of the loose earth as he approached it. He leaned over the cross to examine it further.

"Does it say anything on it?" Verity inquired.

"Yes," he said, leaning further in to read what was very faint lettering. "It's got a name on it."

"What's the name?" she pressed, hugging herself a little from the chill in the air, which suddenly felt colder than before.

Lochlan read aloud, leaning closer to the cross: "Tobe Thacker."

As he recited the name, a pheasant burst loudly from the bushes in the direction they had come from, a few feet away. It let out a terrible cry as it flapped its copper-coloured wings. The bird's plumage flashed in a shaft of yellow daylight as it flew out of the thorns it had been roosting quietly in. In one swift motion it beat its wings and darted through the air towards the tree tops.

The sudden noise caused Verity to spin around in a moment of shock; and as she did, catching sight of the pheasant fluttering upwards, she heard her husband let out a soft gasp behind her.

Verity turned back just in time to see him stumble onto the mound of earth, trying to find his footing, also taken aback by the crying creature. But the soil was looser than it looked; and it began to crumble beneath Lochlan's boots. In one swift fall, he tripped backwards and disappeared into the grave, the muddy mound caving inwards with his weight.

Verity immediately darted over to where he had fallen, presuming she would find Lochlan lying in a shallow ditch. But as she got closer she saw that the grave was deeper than she'd realised. Much deeper.

She peered over the edge of what was, in fact, a resonant hole. So deep, in fact, that she could barely see her husband at all.

Panic in her voice, she called into the blackness beneath her: "Lochlan? Lochlan, are you alright?"

There was a second of silence - which seemed to drag achingly - and then his disembodied voice came up through the hole.

"I - I think so."

He sounded flat and far away. The deeply-dug grave was only the width and length of a small coffin. The narrowness of this hole was keeping his voice muffled. Verity shuddered at the thought of how claustrophobic it must have been down there, especially for her tall, strapping husband, all trussed up in his winter gear.

"Are you hurt?" she asked. "How far have you fallen? I can't see you!"

"I don't know, but it's deep," he called up to her, a twinge of a wince in his voice. "There's no room down here, it's cramped. I guess the earth on each side of me must have broken my fall."

"How far down are you? And are you hurt?"

"I'm not hurt, but this has got to be twenty feet deep."

He sounded fine. But that was quite a fall. And it sounded horribly tight down there, Verity thought.

"How do I get you out?" she yelled down to him, looking into the grave, into nothingness, and feeling ridiculous asking him such a question.

There was a pause. She knew Lochlan; he wouldn't be panicking, he would be thinking of the most logical way to get out. But what that was, she didn't know. And neither, it seemed, did he.

Then he spoke: "Verity, you're going to have to call someone or go and get someone. This is pretty bad, I'm really stuck down here."

She stared into the blackness, towards the sound of his disembodied and uncharacteristically weak voice.

"Um - okay," she answered, blandly.

Remembering she hadn't brought her phone on the walk (why would she need it, she had thought) a flutter of panic rose in her. She tore her stare away from the hole and looked up, back in the direction they had walked.

And then she saw him.

The old man was stood next to a twisted elm. He was small and hunched over. His face was in shadow, but it was undoubtedly the pedlar - the man that had been watching her, naked, that morning from the kitchen window. He carried a bundle of sticks on his bent back and was turned in Verity's direction, looking right at her from the shadows.

She was startled at first, then relieved. Perhaps he could help her.

"Hello?" she called across to him.

He remained motionless, staring back at her.

"Um - hello?" she repeated, waving a little.

No response.

"Who are you talking to?" came Lochlan's voice from beneath.

"Hold on," Verity said, glancing in the direction of the hole before starting to walk towards the pedlar.

His shadowy outline stood amid the dense brush, away from the track that Verity and Lochlan had made as they had headed towards the grave just minutes before. Verity walked towards him, her boots becoming tangled slightly in the catsfoot ivy that layered the copse floor. Rocks protruded here and there as she kicked her way through the undergrowth, stepping over logs and through dried leaves. As she gained on the man, he stayed still, next to the elm, a slight glimmer of his placid eyes visible through the darkness, his cold breath appearing on the air now and again.

"Hello?" Verity called once more, as she navigated her way toward him.

He wouldn't move. He didn't answer her. But she had nearly reached him.

Then, a scream: a shrill, piercing cry rang through the copse, so loudly that Verity stopped and put her hands to her ears.

It came from above her, prompting her to look upwards, through the jagged gaps in the close-knit trees. She saw three pheasants this time, flapping across the break in the treetops. They seemed to be flustered, gathering in the air, wings beating furiously, as if they were fighting. Their screeches, loud and shrill, cut through the air like a steak knife through a buttery filet of beef. They sounded pained and mournful.

With her hands still pressed against her ears, Verity watched the trio of birds as they fought in the air above her, a flap of feathers entangled in what looked like a vicious clinch.

Then, one fell from the sky.

It tumbled, as if it had been shot by a hunter, through the bare branches. It smacked against the craggy boughs of the trees as it fell, limp and lustreless. As it plummeted toward Verity it became caught on one blackened branch which broke its fall. With a tear, one of the bird's wings ripped against the spiky bough, causing the torso of the creature to thwack against the trunk of the tree with a tremendous snap that seemed to echo through the copse. The bird hurtled towards Verity and into her upward-turned face.

She let out a low whimper and stepped backwards as the pheasant's lifeless body slid from her face and landed with a final thud at her feet, its neck snapped at a grotesque angle and its once-beautiful bronze wing disjointed and torn.

She flicked her hair from her face and took a breath, flustered from the sudden encounter with the dead animal, before glancing up in the direction of the old man once again.

He had turned, and was walking away into the trees.

"Wait!" Verity said, more to herself than to anyone else, and started to follow him, stepping over the coppery corpse that lay in the leaves at her feet and spitting a feather from her mouth.

She was flustered and taken aback by the string of occurrences she had gone through so rapidly - Lochlan's fall, the appearance of the man, the violently-killed bird - and now she seemed to be clumsier in her attempts to chase the pedlar. The forest floor appeared to cling on to her boots, with Verity kicking her way through the ivy to get to him. He wasn't walking quickly - he couldn't, he was aged and languid; yet she couldn't reach the man. It felt like a dream in which she was running and running but unable to move.

Ahead of her, the pedlar hobbled along with the bunch of sticks on his back, gliding through the copse, further away from where Lochlan was trapped in the grave.

"My husband - " she tried to call out at the pedlar, only able to gasp her words rather than shout them.

The trees began to thin out a little, and Verity presumed that she had followed the pedlar back towards the clearing. She moved as quickly as she could and, despite her boots being clogged somewhat by the ground beneath her, she appeared to be gaining on him.

Then he stopped. Thank God, Verity thought.

"Excuse me?" she called.

She was tripping slightly through the tangled weeds at her feet, yet getting closer to the man. He didn't turn around, but removed the bundle of sticks from his back, gripping them in his wizened hands.

"I need your help - " Verity breathed, finally within touching distance of the small, hunched figure before her.

And then he turned, raised his bale of twigs and swung them toward Verity as she stepped up to him. She felt the sharpness of the woody sprigs against her skin as the pedlar struck her in the face. She caught a glimpse of his own face. It was the last thing she saw as she toppled backwards onto the frosty ground. His expression was pale, creased and twisted into a gaping, toothless smile.

DECEMBER 10TH.
LAST YEAR.

V erity was fraught with a feeling of terrible unease.
She sat rigidly on the sofa, finding it impossible to lean back for one second. She could not relax. She wouldn't dare.

He was due home. He was due home an hour ago. It could be any second now. Or hours later, even. He was punishing her. He was *forcing* her to wait for him. Maybe he wouldn't come home at all. He wasn't that sort of man - but, this time, he was furious.

She rubbed her palms together tersely. She chewed on her inner-lip, irritated and nervous. Her stomach was in knots. It hadn't helped that she had opted to work from home that day, following the events of the evening before, shutting herself away from life and civilisation, routine and normality. It also hadn't helped that she had done no work whatsoever, and instead obsessed about the situation from the moment Lochlan had left the house without so much as a glance in her direction that morning.

She had nursed a hangover all day - yet, now, wanted another drink. She had walked to the fridge several times but each time had turned on her heel and walked away from it, deciding it unwise to have alcohol on her breath when he came home.

The sound of a gate creaking open from the street above.

She turned on the sofa and glanced out of the frost-smoked bay window across the living room. Her eyes locked widely on the stone steps that led down from the street, down to their front door. She waited for her husband's loafer-clad feet to come into view, and for them to walk down the steps.

Nothing.

The noise of the gate must have been the one next door. It must have been their irritating neighbour coming home. Her gate was squeaky too - much like her voice.

Verity felt both annoyed yet relieved. She wanted this over with yet didn't want it at all.

Her glance jumped from the window to the Christmas tree by the stairs. She had not turned the lights on yet that day - a sign in itself that she was distracted. She stood and walked promptly over to the tree, bending to reach the plug and flick on the lights. The tree lit up, immediately warming the room, offering Verity a small token of comfort.

Standing back, she examined the tree in all its splendour. She admired her own taste in ornaments, and her finesse for decorating. She had gone for a musical theme this year - golden horns, glassy treble-clefs and rolled up scrolls of sheet music tied with emerald ribbon. She really did love this time of year - and was terrified her mistake the night before would ruin it for her and Lochlan.

A gate opening. And footsteps.

He was home.

She remained at the tree-side, partly frozen with apprehension, partly hoping the sight of his wife next to the festive, bedecked spruce would somehow soften him as he came through the front door. She clasped her hands in front of her, then clumsily untangled her fingers again. She placed her arms behind her back, as if she were a handmaid, awaiting the arrival of her master.

The steps shuffled to a halt at the door and there was a pause.

He doesn't want to come in, Verity thought to herself. He doesn't want to see me. He doesn't want to have this conversation as much as I don't want to have it.

She waited. He stood out there so long that the porch light, which came on when someone stepped onto the front step, clicked off again.

Then, a few moments later, the sound of his keys in the lock and the handle turning.

His face was stern. He looked like an angry father, entering his unruly daughter's bedroom to scold her. He stepped into the house and saw Verity immediately across the room, by the tree. He seemed a little startled - probably thinking that she would be hiding somewhere.

But no - there she was. She was sorry, and wanted to prove it the second he arrived home.

He gave her an emotionless look and turned to shut the door.

"Hi." Verity's voice wavered a little.

Lochlan turned back around. He avoided looking at his wife this time, instead heading straight to the stairs.

"Lochlan - "

"I'll be right down and we will talk about this. At least let me put my stuff upstairs please," he interrupted her, stopping on the first step but still refusing to look at her.

"Okay," she replied weakly.

She considered pouring him a drink while he was up there, but, again, decided against it. Alcohol was not required for whatever chat they were about to have. Nor did she want to evoke direct memories of their boozy night twenty-four hours ago.

Yet when he came downstairs minutes later - tie off, top button undone, shirt sleeves rolled up - Lochlan headed straight for the scotch. He clunked an ice cube into a glass, poured a double, downed half of it and stood next to the fireplace.

Verity had, by this stage, returned to the sofa, hoping he would sit next to her on it to talk. But he remained on his feet.

"What the *fuck* did you think you were doing?" he barked, getting straight to the point.

She exhaled, slowly, palms rubbing together once again.

"I don't know. I'm so sorry," she said, finding herself unable to look up at him. "I drank too much."

"Right, so I can't take you to an office party now, at Christmas, in case you get hammered like some teenager and accuse my colleague of adultery," Lochlan asked, his tone soaked in disdain.

She grimaced at this, knowing he was right, and was forced to think back on her behaviour again - a quick flash of Saskia, Lochlan's communications director, appearing in her mind.

She had approached Saskia at the makeshift bar that had been set up for the party, which had taken place at Lochlan's offices. It was an open-plan space, in one of the roomy lofts off Great Swan Alley in The City. The ceiling was a mixture of clear glass and Maplewood beams, the walls panelled, the floor hardwood and glistening. It was very Lochlan. It was corporate-meets-country; industry-meets-outdoorsy; business-meets-pleasure.

It had looked even more splendid bedecked for Christmas: a tall conifer stood at each end of the long office, jam-packed with white lights that reflected on the waxen floors beneath them and the crystalline glass skylights above them; desks adorned with pots of peach poinsettia and clear vases of red amaryllis and cream calla lilies; amber and copper bows hanging from the walls, sweeping dramatically to the office floor.

The "bar" was the conference table, lain out with chunky bottles of spirits, buckets of icy champagne, and carafes of plummy red wine. It had been while stood there that Verity, three sheets to the wind on sloe gin, had come face-to-face with Saskia Warren.

"Hello Saskia," Verity said, coldly, as Saskia reached for a grapefruit martini, freshly mixed by the waistcoat-clad barman the firm had hired for the event.

"Hi Verity. Mrs Tamblyn," was the corrected response.

Why did she do that, Verity had wondered? Why formalise her name like that? Why check herself? Lochlan insisted on a first-name basis at the office, and Saskia had met Verity several times before. The formal front was a guilty conscience, Verity deduced, glaring at the twenty-something cocktail-dress-clad blonde clutching a martini glass in front of her.

Saskia was your typical mid-level millennial: did a degree about social media; used her looks and all the right hashtags to get her noticed by a PR company run by a leering chauvinist called Roger Stunt; left that company three years later when offered a head of communications role at a trendy new company specialising in sports equipment run by a couple of strapping thirty-somethings - Lochlan being one of them.

Verity smiled sourly and said: "Mrs Tamblyn? That's a bit formal Saskia."

"Sorry, I know. Sorry."

She seemed very nervous, thought Verity.

"To tell you the truth, I ate nothing all day because I wanted to fit into this dress and these drinks are going straight to my head."

Verity smiled as sweetly as possible, her own head rocking somewhat thanks to the gin, the faint jazzy Christmas music being played into the room, the warm glare of the freshly-waxed floor, the industrial-style office lighting, and the glimmering tree lights. Each bulb in that room seemed to bounce from every single reflective surface: the tall glass windows, the long shiny floorboards, the copper desk lamps.

Verity felt hot and irritated. Snappishly, she asked Saskia: "Why wouldn't you be able to fit into that dress?"

Verity looked her up and down as she said it. Saskia paused, her lips perched on the edge of the cocktail glass rim.

"Oh, you know. You want to look your best for the office party," she finally said.

Verity smirked. Her eyes left Saskia's porcelain face for a moment and travelled across the office, spotting Lochlan by the printer, chatting with some of his colleagues, listening intently to some man harking on about trekking poles.

After a second, Lochlan's eyes flicked over towards Verity and Saskia. He registered Verity watching him, the mean-spirited smirk still spread across her lips. He shifted slightly and looked back at the pole enthusiast, a slight furrow to his expression as he did so.

Saskia was talking again: "Are you enjoying the party? How's your Christmas shopping going? Are you and Lochlan home for Christmas?"

Verity let out a weak laugh.

"What?" Saskia asked, smiling faintly, unsure of what was funny. "Am I slurring?"

"No, not at all," Verity replied, looking directly at Saskia and bringing her own glass to her lips. "It's just funny that you did that."

"Did what?" Saskia asked, baffled yet still smiling a little, clearly not picking up on the bitter lilt in Verity's voice.

"Called him Lochlan. If I'm 'Mrs Tamblyn', why is my husband just 'Lochlan'?"

Verity took a sip from her gin. Saskia seemed to freeze, perplexed. Then she giggled, nervously.

"Like I said: empty stomach, booze. Not sensible. I blame this dress."

Verity lowered her stare to examine the little black number Saskia was wearing (and wouldn't have had any problems fitting into, even if she had eaten a cheese ploughman's an hour before the party).

"Actually I blame *you*. Not the dress," Verity said, her voice a tad raised; enough that Lochlan looked over again from his spot by the printer.

"Sorry?" Saskia replied after a confused pause, her large round angelic eyes glistening irritatingly in the festively-lit room.

"Are you trying to get him to leave me?" Verity replied, lowering her voice.

The bartender glanced up from the Bloody Mary he was garnishing with pepper and turned away, awkwardly. Verity ignored him. She flicked her eyes away from Saskia to see Lochlan excuse himself from the chat he was having and head towards the two women.

"*Leave* you?" Saskia said, frowning. "I don't...'

She trailed off, lost for what to say to her, clearly wondering whether the whole thing was supposed to be a joke.

Verity gulped. She was feeling dizzier than before.

"Is everything okay here?" Lochlan had appeared next to the women, one hand in his pocket, the other clutching a bottle of beer.

Saskia looked up at Lochlan, innocently. This infuriated Verity for some reason. How *dare* she, she thought.

"Are you fucking her?" Verity asked her husband, in a vicious whisper.

He looked appalled. "Pardon?"

"You heard me."

Lochlan glanced at Saskia who was still clinging on to her martini glass. She appeared to be trembling a little.

It's because they've been caught, Verity thought.

"Verity, what are you playing at?" came Lochlan's bewildered reply.

"Are you fucking this girl? It's not a hard question Lochlan!"

"I'm not, no. What are you *saying* Verity?"

He seemed to be astounded. Maybe she'd got it wrong.

Still, for some reason, Verity pressed on: "I think you're lying to me. Both of you."

Saskia chimed in: "I've said nothing - "

"Quiet whore!" Verity jibed, the words seeming to slice through the office like a cleaver.

Everyone had noticed something was going on now, each guest awkwardly glancing at their drinks, trying not to look. Verity caught sight of one woman mouth the words "don't turn around" to the man she was talking to who had his back to the situation, clearly desperate to see what was happening.

"Verity!" Lochlan boomed.

He was being dominant. He was scolding her. She had made a terrible mistake.

The man with his back turned now spun and stared, Lochalan's loudness making it acceptable for him to look.

Yet Verity still carried on.

"Come on. I'm not stupid, Lochlan. I know things. I know about things." Verity was now slurring. She was making a fool of herself. "And others will know too, won't they? Yes! They will."

The bartender had moved completely away from the drinks table but was watching the drama unfold from the corner of the room. Silence had fallen across the rest of the party, save for the seductive twang of the instrumental saxophone version of Santa Baby that was playing on the speakers.

Saskia - clearly not at all the confident, sassy young bomb-shell Verity had presumed her to be - was staring at the floor, almost terrified to look anywhere else. She still clutched at her martini glass in her trembling hand, as if it were a sacred elixir that she didn't dare to drop.

Lochlan's gaze was now resting firmly on his wife, warningly. He was not a violent man. He was assertive and strong. His look, alone, had a power to it that Verity found incredibly attractive. Yet she wasn't afraid of him. And she was drunk. Drunk and de-fiant and petulant - even though she knew in that moment she had gotten things horrifyingly wrong.

But the petulancy prevailed. Verity turned to the room, and asked loudly: "Are my husband and this woman having sex? Are they? Who knows? One of you must know about it."

Verity searched the room frantically for Lochlan's partner, Charlie. She couldn't see him.

"Where the Hell is Charlie?" she uttered, half-to herself, half-to Lochlan.

The glass door to the balcony opened and two men walked in, having been smoking outside. One was Charlie; the other Verity had never seen before. Noticing the silent room and the performance that appeared to be taking place, Charlie's face, flushed from the cold and the wine, slid into a confused frown.

"What's going on?" he asked, staring beyond Verity to his partner, Lochlan.

No-one spoke.

"Saskia?" the second man from the balcony spoke, again look-ing straight through Verity.

Being ignored riled her even more and Verity asked: "Charlie, are these two fucking please?"

Lochlan closed his eyes, mortified.

"Which two?" Charlie asked, baffled.

"Them! These two! *Them!*" Verity craned her arm around to gesture towards Lochlan and Saskia, without looking away from Charlie, the gin from her glass spilling a little with her brusque movement.

A grin crept across Charlie's face and he glanced back at the other man he'd been on the balcony with, who was looking vague at best.

"Well I hope not," Charlie said, through a chuckle, clearly not comprehending how awkward things had gotten while he had been outside. "Otherwise I won't be going out on the balcony with this guy again. He'll be wanting to throw someone off it."

This broke the tension a tad, and a titter of laughter rippled across the office, the guests thankful for some light relief.

Verity stared past Charlie at the second man who was now smiling nervously, clearly desperate to get over to Saskia and see if she was alright. He was mid-twenties, handsome, athletic and smartly dressed. This was clearly Saskia's boyfriend.

Verity swayed a little from the realisation of what she was doing - and from the mass of eyes that were looking at her, pitying her, laughing at her. She felt Lochlan's furious stare, drilling into the back of her skull. She closed her eyes and turned to him.

"It was Tammy," she whispered to Lochlan, opening her eyes and meeting his stern gaze. "She put the idea in my head."

"We're going home," Lochlan replied.

He brushed past her and marched through the party, his employees nodding sympathetically at him as he walked towards the room where the coats had been hung.

Verity turned to Saskia who was still timidly looking away, clearly wishing the ground would swallow her whole.

"I'm so sorry," Verity whispered.

Saskia looked up and managed a paltry smile. "Merry Christmas, Verity," she said, politely.

Verity turned and walked through the silent room, her shame serenaded by Santa Baby as it came to a smooth climax.

They had gotten into a cab, driven home in silence and Lochlan had slept in the spare room, disappearing in the morning to do damage control.

But now they were face-to-face for the first time since he had disappeared into the guest bedroom nearly twenty-four hours earlier.

"You said last night that Tammy gave you this idea?" Lochlan asked his wife, glaring down at her as she sat on the sofa, speaking to her in the same tone he had as the drama at the party had unfolded.

"Yes," she replied simply.

"Right, so this is all Tammy's fault is it? Is that what you're saying here?"

"No. No, not at all. Last night was my own stupid fault. I shouldn't have listened to her. And I shouldn't have behaved like that."

Lochlan laughed, with irony. He put down his scotch and paced, hands on hips. He looked manly and authoritative - his stone-coloured slacks hugging his strong thighs, his tucked-in shirt accentuating his toned waist, his collar unbuttoned enough to tease the top of his chest. Verity regretted what she had done with every step he took, to-and-fro, across their living room.

He stopped.

"Do you know how humiliating it was for me, walking into that office today?"

"I can't imagine," Verity replied, gingerly, looking at the floor.

"*You* didn't have to deal with it. *You* got to stay here and feel sorry for yourself - "

"I don't feel sorry for my - "

"*You* got to hibernate all day and work on your stupid artsy sketches while I had to face the company - *my* company - and explain to everyone that their boss' wife is not a lunatic and that the whole thing was a misunderstanding.

"Then I had to meet with my lawyer to make sure that Saskia Warren can't file some sort lawsuit against me, or you, or the company. Then I had to have a formal meeting with her. I'm amazed she came in today to be honest, but she did."

Verity felt sick; sick at what she had done to her husband, and sick that he was defending Saskia - regardless of her innocence.

"Those people got an insight into my home life that a boss should never let his employees see," he continued. "I am humiliated."

"Well so am I!" Verity declared, standing. "And I am *so* sorry, Lochlan. I can't believe I did it. Please. Tell me if you can forgive me? Ever? Can you?"

They fell silent.

Lochlan stepped over to the mantelpiece, where he had left his scotch. He seized it irritably and took a long gulp from it as he faced the fireplace, his back to his wife.

There was a further silence. It was tense and awkward. Verity loathed every second of it.

Then, she asked: "You just said those people got an insight into our home life that a boss should never let his employees see. Is that what you think of our home life?"

Lochlan exhaled, but didn't turn around. "You know it's been hard lately," he said quietly.

"Yes. But it's neither of our faults," Verity said to his broad, hunched-over shoulders.

"I know. But Verity - "

"It's been hard for me, too. I want to give you what you want."

Lochlan spun around and came closer to her.

"But it has to be what *you* want, as well," he said.

"It is," she replied, without much conviction. "It is."

DECEMBER 23RD. DUSK

Verity could feel the cold again.

As she regained consciousness and her eyes began to open, she shivered. The bitter air crept across her body slowly as she lay on the frigid, leaf-littered ground of Miser's Copse.

She shuddered and sat up abruptly, her head swimming as she gathered her bearings. She lifted a hand to her cheek and brushed her fingers across it. She felt a scratch; and when she pulled back her hand to look at it, there were flakes of dried blood.

The old man had attacked her.

Fearful that he was still nearby, and suddenly recalling the plight of her entombed husband, Verity briskly got to her knees and looked around the copse, in every direction.

The old man wasn't there. He had gone; and the smoky daylight that had been creeping through the trees earlier was now dimmer. Hours had passed. It was now dusk.

Wrapping her windbreaker around her body, she slowly stood. She had run far enough through the undergrowth to reach the edge of the clearing she and Lochlan had entered before they had veered off into the trees. She turned, trying to decipher how she could get back to the grave and her husband; but the light was already low. She could not decipher which way was the right way to go.

"Lochlan?" she called, pathetically.

Her voice came out as a gruff whisper, deadened by the flat early-evening air that now filled the copse. She looked into the black trees around the clearing that blocked out the dull evening sky as it attempted to bleed through the thick barren branches. A light mist had already begun to form on the damp ground and a whistle of a breeze slithered through the air around her.

"Lochlan."

She uttered it this time, merely stating his name.

✝✝✝

Verity stopped and leant against the tomb-like stone, "Miser's Copse" etched into it, at the end of the path leading out of the trees. She had decided to try to find help. The old man had vanished, having revealed himself to be dangerous. Verity had reasoned with herself that Lochlan was safer in his earthy trap below the ground than she was, alone and exposed. She had decided to go back to The Spinney House and call for help.

She had located the track that led through the trees and out of the copse. As she had dashed along the path, the pine branches had grasped and clawed at her as if trying to hold her back - trying to keep her as the copse's prisoner. She had brushed them off, focusing on getting out onto the surrounding fields. And finally the break in the trees had appeared ahead of her, the glimmer of grey evening light beyond it giving her a little comfort. Verity had broken free of the brambles, which seemed to stretch achingly after her, desperate to entrap her; to keep her for themselves.

She was glad to be out of Miser's Copse. As she leant on the damp stone that sat at the edge of the trees she tried to calm herself a little and to catch her breath.

She looked out at the moors that led back down to the cot-

83

tage. It had snowed lightly during the afternoon - a dusting of white sprinkled around the grassy hillocks like powder sugar on a Christmas cake.

To the left, the pale wintry sun was dipping behind the tree-tops, a slash of cloud running across it like a long tear in a sheet of linen. Small snakes of smoke climbed upward from the direction of Fallows' Spinney, rising slowly from beyond the trees of the woodland that hid the village from view. The sky above the tiny town was already a deep shade of charcoal, one or two stars piercing through here and there.

To the right, down the hill, was The Spinney House - uninhabited, uninviting and dark. It looked bleak on its own at the foot of the hill, no lights in any of the windows. It did not merely adjure the impression of an old, empty house in the middle of rural countryside; it instead seemed colder and more desolate in the dusty evening setting, as night began to crawl in from the surrounding fens.

Nonetheless – this was currently her home. This was where Verity had to go.

Her boots crunching on the frost-laden grass, she made her way down the hill, the white sun behind her, droplets of dew glistening in the grass amongst the low-clinging mist that seemed to have followed her out of the copse.

The wooden gate that opened onto The Spinney House's front path felt wet and rotten under Verity's palm as she pushed it aside to get to the cottage. Having thankfully kept hold of the keys rather than pass them into Lochlan's care, she fumbled in her pocket for them as she stepped onto the porch to unlock the door. Finding them, she inserted one into the keyhole and turned it sharply, the sound of the click cutting loudly through the dense air that surrounded the lonely house.

Verity looked up from the handle - and stopped still.

Hanging on the door before her was the wreath. The same wreath the pedlar had gifted them the day before. The same wreath Verity had stripped from its nail and tossed into the mud. The same wreath Lochlan had discovered that morning, provoking another of their ludicrous jibing matches. The same wreath that was so beyond repair, Lochlan had thrown it away as if it were nothing but mulch.

Yet there it was: hanging majestically on the door once again, looking regenerated and evolved.

It was full and bushy - its mossy base healthy and emerald; the sprigs of cedar looked fresh and outstretched; the sprays of huckleberry and crab-apple were bright and buoyant; the snippings of rosehip were bulbous and flush.

Verity stared at it, one hand on the door handle, the wreath mere inches from her face.

And then a laugh - from somewhere behind her.

She spun around on the doorstep and looked back down the path toward the gate, which was now tapping lightly against its latch in the faint evening wind. Beyond the gate, the moors remained mist-laden and dank, the last of the white sun illuminating rocks here and there. The pathway was dark and empty.

She had heard that laugh - that giggle - somewhere before. Yet nothing was there. And now it was deathly silent.

✠•✠•✠

She perched on the edge of the bed, thinking.

She had been searching for her phone for what felt like several minutes, unable to recall where she had left it. She was sure it had been charging on the dressing table across the room; but the end of the charger lay on the floor, plugged into nothing. Lochlan had most probably taken his phone with him – as stuck down the hole as he was. And the cottage didn't have a landline.

Sat in the small upstairs room, just a lamp on by the bed, the sky outside getting increasingly darker, Verity noticed something behind her light up, on Lochlan's bedside table. It illuminated the corner of the room. It was her husband's tablet with an incoming email notification on the screen.

She leaned across the bed to her husband's side and reached for the device. The screen showed a white box, which read:

From: Ewan McVey

Subject: Squash

Lochlan, just thinking we should book a court if we want to get a match in between now and the New Year, and we also need... [more]

Verity rolled her eyes.

He's on holiday for Christmas, she thought to herself, swiping away the message on the screen and entering Lochlan's pass-code. He's also buried in a grave, she thought, finding herself smirking a little, somewhat inappropriately, brushing one of her black strands of hair behind her ear.

Lochlan's predictably terrain-themed screensaver appeared on the tablet's display - a hazardous-looking mountain trail of some sort – and Verity pushed her finger against the icon for the internet.

Check Connection.

Another annoyance, getting in the way of Verity's attempt to free her husband from his living burial.

The cottage's sporadic wireless signal only seemed to work smoothly in one corner of the living room downstairs, she had learnt over the past few days. It had a tendency to dip out when elsewhere in the cottage. So, she got up and left the room.

As she descended the staircase into the living room of The Spinney House, Verity noticed that she had rushed through the cottage door and up the stairs without turning on any lights. The sun now had fully set outside, and the room had been plunged into darkness.

Tablet in one hand, Verity walked over to the switches on the wall and flicked them on. The room lit up before her - but she was far from comforted. Verity thought about the laughter she had heard on the pathway. She thought about the moors beyond the garden wall - vast and leering. She remembered the man at the window that morning, watching her from outside. She touched her cheek, remembering being struck by him with his bundle of sharp sticks. She recalled the wreath, reattached to the front door, presumably by him.

Feeling exposed, she clicked off the lights and instead moved across the room to the armchair by the fireplace, next to the Christmas tree. She leant down and turned on the lights that bedecked the tree, illuminating the room satisfactorily yet not too garishly.

She sat in the chair, and watched the screen of the tablet, waiting for it to connect to the net. As she waited, she rested her head back. She was feeling tired from what was happening. She remained relatively calm - oddly so - yet weariness was taking over. Her mind began to wander, traveling back over the past few hours. What was the grave in the copse? There was something unsettling about it, and how it had almost appeared like a trap, deep in the trees. Who would want to be buried out there; destitute, almost in exile? Who had marked the grave with the wooden cross? Who was Tobe Thacker?

The internet connected.

Without thinking, Verity was searching the name that had popped back into her head. Momentarily distracted from her husband's current circumstances, she typed "Tobe Thacker Miser's Copse" into the tablet and waited.

After a moment, search results flashed up on the screen, illuminating Verity's face in the otherwise dim corner of the living room.

COPSE NAMED AFTER LOCAL "MISER" TOBE THACKER

Archives > The Stag > News

December 31 1843 > The Squire of Grouse Hall, Mapleridge, has honoured the macabre events of this year's yuletide season by proposing that a copse of trees be planted at the site of the tragedy that took place on...[more]

The news story that sat at the top of the search instantly caught Verity's attention. Without a second thought, she pressed the link on the screen to bring up what turned out to be an archived article from a newspaper called The Stag - presumably Fallows' Spinney's resident rag.

On the screen was a scanned article dated New Year's Eve, 1843. It was a front page piece – presumably important news at the time if it had made the main headlines on the last day of the year - and sat directly under the newspaper's masthead (which was designed in a slanted scrawl, with a logo consisting of a solitary buck deer, stood on a knoll, one leg raised lightly off the ground).

Verity squinted at the screen, trying to make out what the article said, before noticing a link that offered a transcribed, typed version, presumably written up for the purpose of digital digestion. She pressed it and was taken to a block of text, consisting of the article's contents.

COPSE NAMED AFTER LOCAL "MISER" TOBE THACKER

December 31 1843

The Squire of Grouse Hall, Mapleridge, has honoured the macabre events of this year's yuletide season by proposing that a copse of trees be planted at the site of the tragedy that took place on Christmas Day, last week.

Squire Greene learnt of the death of local woodsman Tobe Thacker on Boxing Day, informed of the sinister events during his annual Christmas open house.

The Squire left his guests at his home so he could oversee the investigation that had been commissioned by Chief Constable Lane of the Borough of Mapleridge and Chasterood Constabulary.

A full excavation of the water meadow behind The Spinney

House, Kiln Lane, was carried out, with a concluding report stating that Tobe Thacker had frozen to death after being buried alive on the hilltop.

To mark the tragic passing of the local - who died unmarried with no children, but whose family has roots in Fallows' Spinney and Mapleridge tracing back three centuries - Squire Greene has commissioned a copse of trees that will be planted in the coming spring, to honour Mr Thacker's cruel and unexplained death.

Mr Thacker was known to locals as a "miser" - known to travel door-to-door around Fallows' Spinney selling firewood at seemingly high prices.

As a nod to his notoriety around the region, the copse will be christened Miser's Copse.

The case is being treated as murder, and there are no suspects at this time.

A chill ran through Verity as she reached the end of the article. She lay her head back in the chair once again and thought about what she had just read.

Tobe Thacker had frozen to death after being buried alive on the hilltop.

She thought about the stick that protruded from the loose earth, deep in the centre of the copse, with the name "Tobe Thacker" scrawled into it. She thought about the shallow grave - the grave that her husband was now trapped in. The same grave, she presumed, this old man had been buried alive in, and left to slowly freeze to death in, on Christmas Day over a century ago.

Her eyes travelled back down to the tablet screen and she pressed on it to return to the search results. She clicked on another article from The Stag, this time a smaller entry, less detailed than the one from New Year's Eve. This news story was dated a few days prior to it.

UNIDENTIFIED MAN FOUND DEAD ON MOORS

December 27 1843

The body of a man, thought to be around 75-years of age, has been discovered on the moors surrounding Fallows' Spinney.

He was found in a shallow grave and is thought to have fallen or been pushed. The cause of death appears to be hypothermia.

An investigation has been launched by the Mapleridge and Chasterood Constabulary with the full cooperation of Squire Greene of Grouse Hall.

Any persons with knowledge of the events are urged to come forward.

Verity clicked away from this bulletin. Her mind was troubled by what she was learning. A man had been buried alive on the moors. It stood to reason that this was the same spot she had left Lochlan, the copse evidently planted around it after the death all those years ago.

And the deceased had been a woodsman. A door-to-door seller. A pedlar.

It's not possible, she thought, pushing thoughts of vengeful ghosts from her mind and tapping another link, this time dated in the spring of 1844, a few months later.

VOLUNTEERS COMPLETE PLANTING AT MISER'S COPSE AS MURDER INVESTIGATION CONTINUES

May 3 1844

This week has witnessed the completion of the planting of a new copse on the hill to the south of Fallows' Spinney, henceforth known as "Miser's Copse", in honour of local forester Mr Tobe Thacker, who was killed last year on Christmas Day.

Squire Greene of Grouse Hall told The Stag: "We are happy to mark this poor pedlar's brutal death with this humble coppice. May it grow and thrive and hide away the site of this terrible crime."

Mr Thacker's body was removed from the shallow grave in which he died following an investigation last Christmastide. His corpse was taken to London on January 2, to be examined by Doctor Blake Danner of the Pilgrim's Mortuary, Bread Street, Whitechapel. Doctor Danner's post-mortem report deduced that Mr Thacker had been struck several times over the head. Scratches on his body suggested he had been dragged across rocky terrain and a large wound on his back was likely to have come from being thrown into the hole in which he eventually died. He would have frozen to death, but further examination suggests he may have died from asphyxia, having been buried whilst still breathing.

As Mr Thacker had no living relatives, he was given a pauper's funeral and now rests at Potters Fields Park in Southwark, London. A stone has been set next to Miser's Copse, with the copse's name engraved on it, funded by Squire Greene, as a token of his respect to Mr Thacker's presence in the local community.

The investigation continues.

Verity thought about Tobe Thacker - his body buried, discovered, dug up and eventually re-buried in London, miles from his home, where poverty-stricken, lonely souls were laid to rest after being granted barren, meaningless funerals.

Another article - this time dated the summer of 1844 – caught her attention for even more horrifying reasons. This local tale, it would seem, could indeed get far more disturbing than simply detailing a destitute loner being attacked and left to rot in the ground on the most joyful day of the year.

PARISH VERGER IN POLICE CUSTODY FOLLOWING LOCAL MAN'S DEATH

June 26 1844

A verger from The Church of Abbess Eunice, Fallows' Spinney, has been taken into custody by police under suspicion of committing murder.

Miss Dinah Clarke, 35-years-old, is thought to be responsible for the death of local woodsman Tobe Thacker on Christmas Day last year.

Miss Clarke, of The Spinney House, Kiln Lane, was initially re-strained in the Fallows' Spinney village square on the afternoon of June 24 (Midsummer's Day). She was reported, by a witness, to be "extremely distracted" in the weeks leading up to the summer celebra-tion and was "becoming increasingly distressed" as she oversaw the church festivities in the square on Midsummer's Day. She allegedly became particularly upset when her daughter, Elodie, 12, was an-nounced as this year's so-called Solstice Sire (an honour granted to the child considered to be the most devoted chorister at The Church of Abbess Eunice).

Miss Clarke was not arrested by authorities immediately; she was taken into the local tavern, The Goat, where she was provided with smelling salts to calm down, while Elodie - an only child, whose father died when she was a baby - was taken home and left in the care by another of the church vergers.

Miss Clarke was later sent home to The Spinney House, where she was left with her daughter for the evening. Yet the local constabulary were notified some hours later, by a local shepherd, of a disturbance on the moors behind Miss Clarke's cottage.

On investigation, it was found that Miss Clarke had hiked to the top of the hill that overlooks her home, attempting to uproot the newly-planted saplings on the site.

She was reportedly raving as she did so and described by one of the investigating constables as "highly distraught, almost in a state of violent confession".

It is alleged that the woman was "confessing to all manner of things" - said to be repeatedly muttering about having a child out of wedlock and being a bastard herself. It was here, also, that she im-plicated herself in the death of the late Mr Thacker (whom the copse was planted in honour of in the spring) and was "constantly assert-ing that someone must repent".

As they attempted to placate the woman, other constables investi-gated her cottage, finding her daughter Elodie "calmly sat in the gar-den, wearing her Solstice Sire's crown of elder and oleander, hacking at the earth with a blunt piece of slate".

When asked if she was aware of where her mother was, the girl is said to have merely "nodded and hummed".

The local authorities took Miss Clarke away for questioning and her daughter was sent to the parsonage where she was left with another of the church vergers, as a temporary measure.

It is believed that, since her arrest, Miss Clarke has confessed to being responsible for the sinister live burial of Mr Thacker at Christmastime.

Chief Constable Lane of the Borough of Mapleridge and Chasterood Constabulary is leading the investigation and once again urges any persons with further information to come forward.

A final article seemed to tie the story up in a sinister black bow. Published on the Christmas Eve that followed, it explained the aftermath of the young woman's arrest in 1844 - a year on from Tobe Thacker's death.

"UNASHAMEDLY PIOUS" VERGER RESPONSIBLE FOR LOCAL MAN'S DEATH TO HANG FOR MURDER

December 24 1844

The young woman taken into custody on the moors around Fallows' Spinney on Midsummer's Night has been found guilty of murdering local man, Tobe Thacker.

The trial - which has lasted the entirety of the Michaelmas term at the Royal Courts of Justice, London - was concluded yesterday, December 23, with Justice Sir Adam Honiton finding the church verger responsible for the sinister killing of the wood seller. She was charged with attacking Mr Thacker and taking him to what is now known as Miser's Copse, where she buried him in a shallow grave and left him to die on Christmas Day.

Miss Clarke, 35-years-old, is said not to have directly confessed to the murder, but to have repeatedly insisted that she must be punished for it.

"The lack of discerning evidence in the matter, and the apparent *unsavoury state of Miss Clarke's mental faculties, cast great dubiety in this matter," a court representative told The Stag following the sentencing yesterday. "After what has proven to be a lengthy process, thanks to the ambiguity in the case, it was decided that Dinah Clarke's overriding behaviour be treated as an indirect admission of guilt.*

"Her distracted demeanour since last Christmas, which was attested for by a number of god-fearing witnesses from The Church of Abbess Eunice during the trial, paired with Dinah Clarke's behaviour at the Midsummer festival on the afternoon of June 24, and her attempted-defacement of Miser's Copse hours later, have proven a compelling argument against her.

"There are no other indications that anyone else was involved in this crime. The court has found that Dinah Clarke is guilty of the murder of Tobe Thacker and she will be hanged at Horsemonger Lane Gaol on New Year's Day. Her child, Mistress Elodie Clarke, will continue to be cared for by the church, before she is transferred to an orphanage."

The Stag can reveal that there are plans to re-plant the saplings damaged by Miss Clarke at Miser's Copse. These plans are being overseen by Squire Greene's wife, Lady Victoria Greene, due to her husband's ill health.

Squire Greene reportedly fell into a terrible fever over the summer, when the young woman from his parish was arrested on Midsummer's Night, said to be deeply troubled by the turn of events. Squire Greene and Miss Clarke are said to have been acquaintances due to her diligent involvement with the local church. He is reported to still be extremely unwell.

The screen of the tablet went dark.

Verity sat in the armchair, staring forward, across the room, into nothingness. The glow of the Christmas tree lights somehow gave a morose feel to the otherwise cosy room, the sky now pitch black outside.

The wind had picked up and she listened to it as she sat still in the chair. It swirled around the cottage, curling itself around the corners of the house, moaning like an anguished hag.

Lochlan returned to her thoughts. She remembered him, trapped in the now-dark copse behind the cottage, sure to be colder and more frightened than before. Yet she could not move. She felt unable to get up, to find help, to go outside. She was numb.

A scent of tobacco suddenly wafted over to her as she stared into the darkness. She stayed still in her chair, save for her wide eyes which she moved slowly from side to side, around the room, seeking the sudden source of the smell. Her eyes rested on the chair directly opposite her, across the room, shrouded in shadow. She squinted at it, watching intently for something to happen.

Silence. Just the rich scent, filling the room.

And then, after a moment, smoke began to appear from the darkness of the chair, snaking into the air, grey and wispy.

Then, a voice.

"He died, you know."

Verity knew who was speaking to her from the dark chair. The familiar voice belonged to the pedlar. And she now knew that this was the croaked voice of Tobe Thacker.

"The Squire. He died. He died of disgust."

Verity didn't speak. She did not move. Instead, she kept her eyes on the darkness across the room, where the smoke had now risen into the air and was gathering in a light cloud.

She felt drowsy; it came over her, suddenly. It was as if the day's events were beginning to collapse onto her like some bulbous, abrupt weight; as if rocks were being scattered from above, knocking her shoulders, keeping her down, trapped in her chair by the fireplace. The tobacco smoke wisped from the shadows across the room. It seemed to thicken and fill the air, pungent and oppressive. The bitter aroma teased Verity's senses - her nose tingled and her eyes stung. Her mind, racing just a moment ago, seemed to slow down.

"He died. Of anguish and disgust." Tobe Thacker repeated.

His voice was deadened by the stillness of the room. It was

raspy and aged and, in that moment, lullaby-like.

Verity wasn't falling asleep. Her body felt lax, but she was very much aware; aware that she had been visited, again, by something terrible and sallow. This time, it was not on the path or at the window, but inside The Spinney House, keeping company with her in the dim room.

This man - this ghost - was no longer tempting her with trinkets from the forest and promises of a happy, festive Christmas. He was there to offer her something else instead: a first-hand account. A report; not merely pieced together by titbits from the local rag.

Verity felt as if she were between worlds. She was neither fully alert nor dozing. It was as if she were under a spell. His spell.

Whether this apparition was indeed sat with her in the low-ceilinged room, she didn't truly know. Yet, she sat and listened to it speak.

TOBE THACKER.

V erity still could not see his face. All that came from the darkness across the room was smoke, creeping slowly into the glow of the Christmas tree's lights, carrying with it Tobe Thacker's disembodied voice.

Still in her drug-like state, Verity did not feel afraid. Her heart was thudding in her chest but it wasn't a frightened thud. It was nervousness, intrigue, concern. But she was not afraid.

"Who are you?" she asked, timid yet inquisitive, her own voice sounding somewhat unattached, far away.

A wheezing laugh from the chair.

"You know," came the raspy answer.

She did know.

"You're dead," she stated.

With this, movement came from the chair. Tobe Thacker shuffled forward, out from the darkness, leaning into the light glow of the Christmas tree. His pallid face was twisted into a macabre grin. His wizened skin's creases looked deeper and more defined in the lowly-lit surroundings. His aged body struggled to sit forward, but he moved a little to the edge of the chair, raising one of his hands to his mouth, holding a pipe in it. He sucked on it, inhaling wetly before grinning again, allowing smoke to seep past his one crooked tooth.

Verity didn't want to look at his twisted face, but could not draw her gaze away from it. She was repulsed yet intrigued by him all at once.

"Did you like my wreath?" he asked her, smiling still.

She nodded, unsure of what else to do or say.

"Your husband didn't," he observed, his eyes darkening a little.

Verity finally tore her stare away from his face. She was ashamed of Lochlan for turning the man away when he first knocked at the door two days ago. She was embarrassed that her husband had tossed the wreath away with the rubbish that very morning.

Tobe watched her, taking another sickly puff of his decrepit-looking pipe.

"My husband is in trouble," Verity said weakly, suddenly finding words.

Tobe sucked in some more smoke and nodded. "Yes. He is."

"Can you help him?"

"He is in the copse," Tobe stated before ominously adding: "He is in the grave."

This sent a chill through Verity, but she nodded in agreement.

"He's buried in the grave," Tobe reiterated.

"He fell. He fell into your grave," Verity said.

The incessant smirk on Tobe's face vanished as she said these words and he lowered the pipe away from his mouth briskly.

"*My* grave?" he asked her. "No. It isn't *my* grave."

Verity thought back to the newspaper articles, and how this man, who had no money nor any family, had been given a pauper's funeral, buried in London. How insensitive she must seem, she thought, referring to the spot in which he was left to die - slowly and painfully - as his place of rest.

"I'm sorry," she said, with honest remorse.

His expression was one of malice and he raised his pipe again, taking a deep inhalation and pursing his lips tightly.

"Is it not your husband's grave now?" he asked her, spitefully.

Verity moved for the first time since her sudden encounter with the visitor.

"No, I need to get him out," she said, sitting upright in the armchair.

"Should not the lex talionis be applied to those who have so often made themselves merry at our expense?" he asked her.

"Pardon?" she responded, genuinely unsure of what he was getting at, his words dancing around her somewhat blithely.

"Measure for measure," he said, bluntly.

"My husband should not be left in that ditch to die. He hasn't done anything to deserve it," Verity declared, feeling suddenly impassioned.

"Has he not?" Tobe asked her, taking another suck of the blackened pipe.

"No!" she asserted, her words echoing in her own head, still feeling somewhat light-headed, as if the whole thing were a hazy hallucination. She gripped the arm of her chair to steady herself, as if she could fall out of it at any moment.

"He turned me away at the door. An old pedlar trying to sell him some humble trinkets of the season. He turned me away on a frozen winter's day, at Christmastide no less," Tobe said.

"I'm sorry he did that," she answered, genuine in her sentiment. "But I have more than made up for it."

At this, she pointed at the bough of spruce that lined the mantelpiece above the fireplace, sold to her previously by the man that was now sat opposite her in the living room.

As she looked in the direction of the mantle, she froze. The garland seemed to have thickened somewhat - it had grown. Much like the rejuvenated wreath that had been re-nailed to the front door, this garland appeared to have flourished and germinated, now trailing down each side of the fireplace.

She looked around at the rest of the greenery the pedlar had sold to her - the boughs on the banister, the sprigs of pine across the top of the dresser, the firewood stacked in the grate.

It had changed - all of it. It seemed to have thrived and propagated as if it were still rooted outside in the thick landscapes of the moors and the forests. The bough that crept up the banister appeared to have tripled in size and length and slithered up the balustrade like an olive-green adder. It almost appeared to move, reaching up and up the bannister towards the top of the stairs, entwined around the wood like a long snake wrapping itself around a helpless deer. The birch wood stacked by the hearth looked damp and mossy. Its silvery bark glistened in the sallow glean of the Christmas tree lights. The moss looked black and morose, clinging dankly to the sodden wood like cockles to a rock by the seashore. It looked like it was breathing; it was like it had seeded and grown.

The whole scenario was unnerving and grim; yet Verity, still in her trance-like state, was still not afraid.

"I thank you for your generosity," Tobe said, acknowledging the seasonal flourishes around the room that had somehow developed their own auras. "But that was *your* generosity, Verity."

He had not yet spoken her name, and her attention once again turned back to the man sat across from her.

"I am not the only person your husband has wronged," he continued. "What about what he did to *you?* With Tammy."

The fact that this man knew about Tammy did not surprise her. Nor did the fact that he knew Verity's name. This man was no longer a man. He was dead. He was a relic, a spectre. He was over a century old. Reasoning was fruitless.

"That happened because of what *I* did," Verity replied.

"And then?" he asked.

"Then... what?" She was unsure what he could mean.

"You made a mistake; he made a mistake," Tobe Thacker continued. "His mistake was far graver than your own. And so...?"

Verity stared at him, waiting for the words - *those* words - to be thrown at her from his spiteful lips once again.

"So: you killed her."

There they were. The words she was expecting. And, like the day before, he said them with a delighted malice that sent a cold rush through Verity's body, like a wintry gust of wind skulking through the bracken in the woods outside. And once more, just as she had yesterday, she felt baffled by how he could have possibly known what she had done. Yet somehow, this time, it seemed more reasonable that he could know of her terrible secret.

"You killed her." He repeated it once more, the spindly grin prowling across his mouth again.

"Yes. I killed her!" Verity agreed. "I killed Tammy!"

He rocked forward all of a sudden - the spriteliest movement she had seen him make - and he clasped his hands together delightedly, a gasp escaping his mouth. His grin became a wide-open smile, his mouth a cavern of blackness, his single tooth poking grotesquely out from his grey gums.

"And...?" he asked.

Verity waited.

"And you were *right* to kill her!" Tobe said, just as he had done on the garden path the afternoon before. "One less whore in this world."

She watched him as his expression darkened again and he sunk back into his hunched position in the seat, recoiling his crooked body once more.

"One less jade in this unholy world," Tobe muttered this time, more to himself.

Verity desperately wondered what had happened to him; what he had done to be killed so brutally by the young woman - a woman of God - who lived in the very house they were now sat in. She ached to know.

Another jolt of disconcertion seeped through her. For the first time since she had learned about the miser's death, it dawned on her that she had been staying - living, sleeping, making love - on the very site of the appalling events she had read about. She had hiked on the same moors this man had been buried beneath, only to be exhumed and sent to a mortician's block in a city far away.

She felt suddenly enveloped by a calignosity that bit at her from all angles, like a pack of spleenful rats. She didn't know whether it was the house, or the very land the house sat on; whether it was the ghost of Tobe Thacker or the ghost of the lunatic woman that had buried him alive in 1843. Perhaps it was merely the feelings inside *her*: the feelings she had swallowed and had been trying to keep down for days, like bile churning within her gut, desperate to rise.

Tobe's reminder to Verity of what she had done to Tammy, the night before she and Lochlan left for Fallows' Spinney, was causing the dam inside her to wane and bend. It creaked and cracked with every breath she took. It was babbling in her stomach and she was suddenly more aware of it than ever before. She was in a place or darkness. There was evil around her - her own nefariousness the most troubling of all - and it was taunting her inner guilt, beckoning for it to come out of hiding and face the world. She had swallowed it, and now it was scaling her innards, trying to break her.

"They called me the miser. The miser in the wood," Tobe said, solemnly.

Verity had stopped paying him any attention for the past few moments and the room had become very still. She glanced back at his chair and saw that he had slunk back into it, his face mostly covered in shadow once again. The slight sheen to his waxen, sickly skin could be made out through the gloom, his hollow, sloe eyes peering frighteningly back at her.

"I lived in a hut in the forest between here and the village. I lived a meagre existence at the end, really," he said softly, his voice less bitter, more anguished. "I didn't always. I was happy as a young man. I worked as a gardener at Grouse Hall, over the hill. I had a sweetheart. Jolette. Jolette Lavinia Clarke."

Tobe's lulling voice had allowed Verity to relax a little, confident that she would be able to sit and gather her wits as he told her his story. Yet the last word caused her ears to prick, like a hare's in March at the sound of a shot.

Clarke.

That name. She knew it.

Miss Dinah Clarke, 35-years-old, is thought to be responsible for the death of local woodsman Tobe Thacker on Christmas Day last year.

She recalled the newspaper articles she had read about the miser's killer.

Miss Clarke, of The Spinney House, Kiln Lane.

Verity now understood that she had been residing in the home of Tobe Thacker's killer, Dinah Clarke. Jolette - Tobe's lover - must have been her mother.

"Jolette was a seamstress. Well, rather a spinner. Her mother was originally from France, but she had married an English miller. The mother died young and Jolette was raised solely by her father at his watermill in Chasterood. He taught her how to spin and, thanks to his relationship with Grouse Hall - delivering flour for the Squire and his family - they employed her to spin wool for the household. Wool for clothing, for bathing cloths, woollen coverings for the beds at the Hall.

Squire Phene - the Squire when I was a young man - was so impressed with Jolette's skill that he asked her to spin a tapestry for his wife's Christmas present one year. It was around this time they moved her here. Into The Spinney House."

Through the gloom, Verity watched Tobe's black eyes travel upwards, towards the low, beamed ceiling. He was silent for a moment. Verity looked up too. She was aware once more of the wind outside the cottage, curling around the house as if it were a skulking thief, searching for a way to get inside in order to loot from them.

The house seemed to tilt slightly. It didn't really, of course, but Verity still felt unsteady, as she had done when she'd clutched on to the arm of the chair for support a few minutes earlier.

Tobe seemed to be waiting. Listening. He watched the ceiling above him, the ornaments from the tree casting glassy shadows across it. The wind moaned from outside, the few dry leaves that still clung to the garden trees rustling on their boughs. The sycamore at the side of the cottage scraped against the chimney breast. The whole house seemed to creak morosely.

Tobe was behaving as if someone would appear; as if he were expecting a visitor. It was as if he were a father, listening out for the sound of a sleeping child, stirring in a bedroom upstairs.

But nothing.

He looked back through the gloom at Verity again, and then spoke brusquely at her.

"We *were* sweethearts!" he snapped at her, as if she had tried to contradict him. But she had said nothing. "Jolette loved me! She did!"

Verity remained silent and listened to him speak, partly to her, partly to someone or something that she couldn't see. Whether it was Tobe's ghostly state or Verity's own foggy disposition, it felt that there was another presence with them in the room, arguing with the miser as he tried to carry out his haunting.

Staring straight into Verity's face, the ghostly man continued: "They said I had delusions, you see. They said I was obsessed. They tried to insist I only loved her from afar. That was not true. She loved me too."

Verity didn't believe him. He was clearly an erratic man in his youth, as well as his eventual old age. She begun to understand that his character would lead to his murder. Yet she still didn't know precisely how this had happened.

"Jolette and I would exchange pleasantries at Grouse Hall. She would enjoy the gardens - *my* gardens - when she would step out in the afternoons after a morning at the spinning wheel in the scullery, off the kitchens. This was before she was moved to The Spinney House and was still living at her father's mill. She worked there every day. And I always watched her at her loom when I would come to the kitchens with herbs and vegetables from the grounds.

The summer she began at the Hall, the cook, Bunty Margaret, jested with me that it was shame Jolette did not weave baskets, too. More for me to carry the fruit and vegetables with, seeing as I was constantly back and forth from the orchard and the vegetable plots. But the truth is I simply made more trips inside, with the hope that I would speak to Jolette one day.

"She did speak to me once, as she strolled around the east lawns of the Hall after her morning's work, admiring the wild flowers that grew there. She had startled me as I was sowing seeds of forget-me-nots. It was September and she had been drawn to the apple trees that were early that year. She spotted me and asked if she may taste one which I, of course, agreed to.

"I was elated to have finally conversed with her. But my hopes of a friendship with her were somewhat stunted when Squire Phene decided to move Jolette closer to the moors. His estate included The Spinney House - this very house - and he felt Jolette required somewhere away from her father's mill and the scullery in which she could work and live. It was closer to the shepherds who reared their sheep on the water meadows and provided her with the wool she needed for spinning. And she deserved it, the Squire said.

"By Allhallowtide of that year she had been moved into this cottage, and was set to work on the tapestry she was looming for the Squire's wife. She stopped working from the Hall. I seldom saw her.

"That Christmas - the Christmas of 1799 - I plucked up the courage to pay Jolette a visit, to wish her the best of the season. It was a harsh winter and snow had fallen the night before. The roads from Chasterood - I still lived in the grounds of Grouse Hall at the time - were tough, but I set off in the morning and made it to The Spinney House in good time, before it became dark in the mid-afternoon. I recall snow clouds gathered once again as I was made the journey, but I didn't, for one moment, consider turning back. I had a winter pudding for Jolette and so desperately wanted to see her.

"As I eventually arrived on Kiln Lane I remember feeling like a child on Christmas Eve. I was instilled with a joy I had not known to feel before. This was not merely a seasonal jollity, rather a nervous elation. I approached The Spinney House from around the crook in the lane and my heart leapt as I saw smoke rising from the chimney and the flicker of candlelight in the front window."

Tobe stopped again and tore his eyes away from Verity, glancing from side to side.

"This very room," he muttered, with an air of suspicion and

caution.

Verity took a breath. She could sense what was coming. Jolette Clarke never loved Tobe Thacker. They barely ever met. He was obsessed with her from afar and, what happened next, would lead him down a destructive, unhealthy and frightening path.

"As I opened the gate, my legs weak from nervosa, clutching that winter pudding all wrapped up in brown paper with a string bow and a sprig of holly in it from the topiary maze at Grouse Hall, I made out Jolette in the window. Her silhouette against the flickering candlelight. I was elated to see her at first, but then realised - she was undressed.

"Mortified, of course, I looked away, praying to God she had not seen me, lest she be embarrassed. But as I turned to retreat back down the path, I noticed a pony and cart in the cottage yard. She already had company."

Verity listened intently, despite, somehow, knowing precisely what would come of this tale.

"I am ashamed to admit that I briskly turned to look back inside the house," Tobe went on. "She was not alone inside. She was naked, with a man. And as I peered through the window as best I could from the path, I saw that it was the Squire. She was bare-breasted in his arms. He too was unclothed. He kissed her neck as she clutched the back of his head.

"I understood. The Squire had been just as besotted with Jolette as I had been. He had sent her to live in The Spinney House so he might steal away and be alone with her. He knew they would always have privacy there as he owned this cursed place.

"They made love. I watched them. As the oily white sun disappeared behind the storm clouds that afternoon, I disguised myself in the darkness. I crept into the garden and stood before the window and watched Squire Phene - the pig - as he skewered my beloved before my very eyes, the newly-woven tapestry Jolette had spun for his ignorant wife strewn over the table across the room. The tapestry he would take home and present to her a few days later for Christmastide."

Tobe Thacker's voice was full of disdain. Disgust.

"I watched from outside in the bitter cold, as it began to snow, still clutching that wretched pudding in my shivering hands," he went on. "I watched as the Squire fed Jolette's dumb glutton before my very eyes. I watched as she writhed before him against that very window!"

He flicked his hand up and pointed one spindly finger over his shoulder, without turning his head. It was the window Verity had knelt in front of, on the very chair Tobe now sat, as Lochlan had pleasured her the night before. She looked past the old man and at the glass, still smeared with her dried saliva from where she had sucked at the condensation in her moment of thirst.

Her eyes fell back down to meet Tobe's, who was staring at her with knowing vitriol. She knew it had been this sour old miser who had watched her and Lochlan the night before - just as he had watched Jolette and her lover all those years ago.

A sudden rush came over Verity as she realised how nonsensical the whole scenario was. She *had* to be dreaming by now, she thought. She knew the encounter with the ghost was not a fully-conscious one; yet she knew it was, indeed, happening.

"I waited in the lane that night for Squire Phene to leave The Spinney House," Tobe said. "For him to finish having his way with my Jolette and go home to his wife."

My Jolette? But she wasn't *yours* was she Tobe?

Verity thought this, but dared not say it. Yet, as if he could tell what was going through her head, the old man glared wildly across the room at her. She felt oppressed again: by him, by the house, by the throbbing greenery that decorated the room and by whatever second spectre she believed lurked in the shadows.

Who else was with them? It wasn't Jolette, Verity thought. Was it Dinah Clarke? She could not tell.

"It goes without saying that I did not return to my position at Grouse Hall," Tobe continued. "A smarter man might have gone back to keep a close eye on the Squire. A smarter man might have returned and told the Squire's wife what her husband had been doing with the household seamstress. But I could not leave my beloved. I had to be constantly close to Jolette.

"And so, that night, after I watched the Squire's cart disappear up the lane away from The Spinney House, I left my packaged gift on the doorstep for Jolette, without a note, and vowed to myself that I would always be close to her.

"That's when I ventured into the woods and decided to live there. I collected wood and I built myself the home - the shack - which I would live in for the rest of my life, just a mile away from this very cottage.

"The forest was the best place to live. To hide. It was sheltered and provided solitude and a place in which to retreat. The copse, of course, did not exist yet. Not until after my death."

He stopped for a moment, thinking. About his death, Verity presumed. Then he continued.

"I remember watching from the lane the next morning, sodden from spending the night gathering wood in the snow, as Jolette opened the cottage door and found my parcel. My pudding. Her smile alone made my Christmas a merry one. I knew she had not wanted to be taken by the Squire. He will have forced himself onto her. And she would have felt obliged, as she was in his employ and indebted to him for the roof over her head. And although he came back, again and again, as the months rolled on, and she let him inside her home and inside her body over and over again, I knew she did not have a taste for it. It was lewd. She was too pure for it.

"She acted her pleasure. It was pretence on her part. I just know it. I would always watch when he visited and logged when he left. And I would always reward her with a gift the next morning. I would quietly leave something for her - a posy of wild poppies, or a dolly I would fashion out of straw, or a gathering of blackberries from the bush in the lane. It was a way of repaying her for what she would have endured the night before with the sweaty old hog of a Squire.

"I would always leave him something, too. I would skin a rabbit and leave it bloodied at the grand entrance of Grouse Hall.

It would be a mammoth undertaking to travel there and back to deliver this every time he visited Jolette, but once I began I could not break the pattern. He had to know that what he was doing was corrupt and wrong, and that every time, the next day, he could expect something. A sign. A token - as if delivered by Satan himself, gifting him for his adultery, honouring him for defying God. These were omens. It was up to me to deliver them.

"I became ill, however. Living off the land, barely nourishing myself, keeping a vigil on The Spinney House, trekking to and from Chasterood at least once a week. It became draining and, despite being a young man of 27, I turned frail before my years. I had to, therefore, stop.

"For several months I tended to myself, alone, in my shack in the forest, surviving on very little and nursing myself to a state of health that I felt acceptable, in order to continue what had become my mission. Yet when I felt well enough to return to The Spinney House the following spring, to see my love, I learned that she had birthed a child.

It was, of course, the Squire's. A bastard girl child. I learned of her when taking my first full walk to the house from the woods, just to get a glimpse of Jolette after so many months away from her.

"I got that glimpse; yet not the one I had imagined. Joelette was outside in the sunshine, cradling her baby as she sat on the cottage lawn. She cooed over it. And as I peered through the local hedgerows to watch, I heard that she called it Dinah."

Miss Dinah Clarke, of The Spinney House, Kiln Lane.

Verity's eyes widened a little as the pieces of the story began to finally fall into place.

Miss Dinah Clarke is thought to be responsible for the death of local woodsman Tobe Thacker on Christmas Day last year.

This child - this baby - would grow up to kill the miserable man now sat before Verity.

How Tobe Thacker must have despised that child, both in life and now in death; the lovechild of his obsession and her swain.

Verity knew that this "hog of a squire" (as Tobe put it) had not forced himself on Jolette. She had been happy as his mistress.

"It was not his child!" Tobe squawked brashly from his dingy corner, again as if he was reading Verity's thoughts. "It was *mine. My* rightful child."

She didn't respond to this; merely sat and waited for his ludicrous reasoning.

"The seed might have been Squire Phene's but, no. He was absent. He came and went. He came, had his way with Jolette, cooed uninterestedly over Dinah and left them for another week. It was *me* watching over them. From afar, perhaps. But every day I would visit the cottage, in hail, snow or baking summer heat. I left gifts for Dinah. Lamb's milk, honey, a toy jester I stole from a stall in Fallows' Spinney on market day. I provided for that child more than Squire Phene did. He might have fathered the bastard thing and kept them in this house, but I was the true father."

Verity wondered whether Tobe Thacker had ever even held the child. His obsession had only been from a distance. Was this man so deluded that he could possibly believe what he was saying?

"The Squire had to go. And he did. Eventually."

Verity spoke for the first time in what felt like hours: "Where did he go?"

Her voice reverberated inside her head. It caught her off guard. She was still in the strange trance-like state as this maudlin tale was being spun in front of her, and had been listening to it in silence. Yet she felt compelled to press Tobe Thacker for answers. His delusion had led her to feel a contempt towards him that he should be questioned about.

"Where did the Squire go?" she asked again.

Tobe's eyes narrowed in the darkness and he glared out at his one-woman audience.

"Died. He died," he hissed.

"How?" she asked, brazenly.

She made out the crooked smile as it returned to the miser's pallid face, shrouded in gloom, slithering slowly across his thin lips.

"I killed him," he growled, proudly. "I was right to kill him."

The words. *Those* words.

You killed her. You were right to kill her.

She knew why Tobe Thacker held Verity in high regard for killing Tammy. It was the same reasoning he had used on himself when he was a young man, to kill his love rival. Yet these people - Jolette and the Squire - did not know of him. He was as much a ghost to them, in life, as he was now, in death.

"I killed him on the very lane he travelled along every week to visit Jolette and Dinah," Tobe went on. "It was the day Dinah turned one-year-old. I knew he would be coming to deliver her his false affections. And so I waited, at the bend in the lane, on the edge of the forest, for his horse and trap. And as it came up the lane I set alight a faggot of sticks and threw it into the horse's path.

"The creature whinnied and reared. It was majestic. It was a sight to behold as it overturned its own trap and sent the fat Squire rolling out, onto the grit, where I crawled from the hedgerows, grabbed at his legs and pulled him into the under-growth.

"This is where I took a rock and brought it down on his ro-tund, distressed face. I wiped the smirk off it, once and for all. I killed him. And I was right to. For Jolette and for Dinah.

"He recognised me, too. It had been a long while since I had retired from my job at Grouse Hall, and he most probably had forgotten my face. Yet, in that moment, before I took his life, he recalled. It was a relishing moment, I tell you Verity."

The ghost spoke to her as if they were comparing notes. Notes on murder.

"I set alight to the body in the woods and let it roast while I picked wild summer flowers and wove a funeral wreath with them. Not for him - for Dinah. For the daughter he was leaving behind.

"I left the wreath on the door of this cottage, for Dinah's birthday. Her father never came to The Spinney House that day. But I did. I looked out for Dinah and her mother."

Verity frowned at the delusion of it. Tobe Thacker had taken so much from this woman and her child, for his own selfish reasons. Yet he could not see it as anything but an act of twisted redemption.

She thought of him lurking in the trees of the forest, waiting for the clip-clop of the Squire's horse on the rocky lane. She pictured him lighting his clasp of sticks and hurling them through the trees at the poor creature. Watching with the same overjoyed, open-mouthed expression she had seen on his face earlier as the horse had bucked and tossed the Squire. She imagined Tobe - deranged, obsessed Tobe - crawling like a goblin out of the bracken to grasp at the Squire's limbs and pull him into the woods, like Grendel stealing the gentry and hauling them back to his swamp.

She imagined the Squire's body, on a bed of dried leaves, in flames behind Tobe, while he gleefully sewed together the funeral wreath for Dinah. She pictured him nailing the wreath to the door of The Spinney House, just as he had done days ago at the same door, but with a Christmas wreath. That time, it had been for Verity, she thought. She felt another chill, as if a droplet had fallen from an icicle and was trickling down her spine.

"Of course no-one ever knew what came of Squire Phene, but me," Tobe said. "But I kept watching Jolette and Dinah, who were gifted this house by the Squire's ignorant wife, Lady Phene. She did not know that Dinah was her missing husband's bastard child, but took over the household accounts and kept Jolette on as the spinner for Grouse Hall, until, eventually, the new Squire, Squire Greene, took over. Lady Phene saw to it that Jolette remained in the employ of Grouse Hall after she left, and that her right to The Spinney House stayed intact, unaware of Jolette's involvement with her mysteriously-missing and presumed-dead husband.

"And so Jolette stayed here, and raised Dinah under this roof. She lived her life believing that Squire Phene had either run away or been accosted by a highwayman and was long killed. And Dinah never knew him. He was merely mulch, left rotting in the dirty leaves on the forest floor. I knew this. No-one else did."

He smiled at this, pleased with himself, before going on: "I continued to watch over them both, from afar. I had even planned to, one day, speak to them. To be welcomed by them, somehow. But I had become so very accustomed to being on the edge of their lives, rather than a part of them. So I kept a steady distance.

"Years passed like this. I became a forester. I provided fire-wood for Fallows' Spinney. It hardly reaped much in the way of reward but I only lived a simple life. And I dedicated myself to providing only for Jolette and Dinah, who continued to be none-the-wiser to whom their silent benefactor was - not that I was able to gift them with much.

"I grew into middle-age, as, of course, did Jolette; Dinah became a woman. And while I still loved Jolette, it had become an almost paternal love for them both. I watched her tutor Dinah at spinning. I decided to fashion her a spinning wheel out of wil-low wood.

"But there was no need after Jolette became unwell. Dinah would use her old wheel, and I would see less and less of her mother. She would stop taking a turn around the gardens in the evenings. She would not sit out in the shade of the sycamore any longer in the summers. I would barely catch a glimpse of her through the parlour window anymore. She became confined to her bedroom upstairs and I would never, ever, see her. I missed her, desperately.

"It became too much for me to bear eventually and one September afternoon, when I was in my fiftieth year, I did something I had not ever dreamt I would - nor could - bring myself to do.

"While Dinah - by that stage a woman in her twenties - was out at the village for the afternoon, I let myself into The Spinney House. This house.

"It was the first time I had ever set foot inside. I remember the way it felt to hear the latch on the unlocked cottage door as it opened, and to step into this very room. The scent of it hit me: rose-hip and marjoram. Perfume. The scent of two sweet women.

"I spent time in this room first of all. I savoured it. I stood at the window I had looked in through that freezing afternoon, as I'd watched Jolette rut with the Squire. It filled me with desire and disdain and a sanguine nostalgia, all at once.

"And then I had gone to the staircase and climbed it. Slowly, one step at a time, getting ever-closer to Jolette, my love.

"I found her asleep in a bedroom. Sound asleep. She lay with her hair across her face - now with flecks of grey in it, like mine. She now had small creases around her eyes and her mouth. She was breathing slowly and softly. There was a slight gruffness with each breath. A rattle. It was her illness - whatever that was.

"I sat with her, next to her as she slept. I touched her. I stroked her face and her hair. She did not stir. She seemed, somehow, to sleep sounder. I imagined laying with her. I imagined holding her. And so, I did. I curled myself around Jolette, next to her. I lay behind her and pressed my chest into her back as it moved with each quiet breath. And I too fell asleep.

"I was woken, however. Abruptly. Not by a sound or a movement, merely by a presence. I opened my eyes and felt that Jolette and I were no longer alone. And so, with my love still sound asleep next to me, I rose to see Dinah in the doorway.

"She had returned home and was stood, still, a look of horror on her face. She had one hand to her mouth and fret in her eyes. And, without a word, she turned and ran down the cottage stairs.

"I heard her leave the house through the front door. I got up and went to look out of the window, down to the lane. Dinah ran up the garden path and through the cottage gate. She dashed along the lane to where a young man was wheeling a cart stocked with straw bales from the late harvest. Dinah, hysterical, appeared to implore him to follow her back to the house.

He brought his scythe with him from shredding the wheat, and ran after her.

"Naturally, dread filled me. I was now a man of middle-age, and weak from my meagre existence. I could not match the brute strength of a land-working youth. Yet, I was overcome with fury. Dinah - who I saw as my own child - was frightened by me. I had simply wanted to rest alongside her mother - the woman I loved, and had done for decades. The woman I had saved from life as a mistress by ridding the world of her debaucher.

"I turned to look at Jolette, still sleeping silently. She was so sick that even this activity had not woken her. I heard the urgent steps on the gravel of the garden path; heard the cottage door slam and two sets of feet climbing the stairs of The Spinney House, hurriedly.

"With a final sad glance at Jolette I turned to the door as the farm boy arrived at the doorway, brandishing his scythe, an anxious look in his eyes. As he saw me, his stare softened, clearly unimpressed by the threat he was faced with. Unimpressed with me: weak, austere, raw-boned. No match for a strapping young farm lad. He wore his shirt-sleeves rolled up, his forearms glistening with mucky sweat from his work in the fields. He wore a red kerchief around his forehead, his strawberry blonde hair flopping over the top of it, matted to his bronzy skin from his dash into the house. His narrowed eyes were bright with the energy of youth. He was alive with the glean of a man who had grown up working in the fields, in the elements, with the earth. Much like I had, myself. Only I had spent the past thirty years returning to a shack in the forest at the end of each day, barely retreating to an actual home to rest my head. This boy, evidently, had a sturdier roof to go back to at night.

"Dinah stood behind him in the door, her fretful eyes snapping from me to her invalid mother in the bed, and back at me again. I moved, suddenly. The lad bared his teeth and gripped the scythe in his strong fists. Dinah drew herself closer to him and clutched one of his arms from behind him. She was terrified of me.

"'Pardon the intrusion,' I said. It came out croaked and haggard. I seldom spoke aloud and it startled me how aged my own voice sounded. 'I meant no harm to your mother.'

"The lad spoke: 'Sir, you must leave this house. We don't want no trouble.'

"I nodded, solemnly. I looked back down at Jolette - still asleep.

"'Rest well, my love.' I whispered it, but they heard.

"'Your *love*?' Dinah asked, her voice full of accusation.

"'You must leave sir. Get out, if you please,' the lad said, his widened stare affixed on me as if I were a lunatic wielding a cleaver, about to strike the sleeping lady in the bed at any moment.

"Yet it was Dinah I was looking at, full of affection and malice all at once.

"'Yes,' I answered her. 'My *love*!'

"My inflection was bitter; and it caused the farmhand to step forward, lifting the scythe a little.

"'I'm warning you old man,' he said, his chest puffed like a protective wren.

"I remember it stinging me, like the nettles I was so used to traipsing through in the woods day in, day out. *Old man.* I may have only been fifty, but I knew I was older than my years, in so many ways.

"I noticed the looking glass across the room for the first time and glared at myself in it. The man staring back at me was not the man I recalled. He was hunched and spindly. He was worn and tattered. He had lost teeth and hair. He was only fifty-years-old, yet looked seventy. He was a wretch; an abomination.

"The sight of myself angered me; and in an act of defiance, as if it were the last thing I would do, I bent to lay a kiss on Jolette - her skin as sallow as my own beneath my brittle lips.

"This jolted the young couple in the doorway, the lad moving toward me suddenly; and in a spritely move I jounced across the bed chamber to the small window, which was ajar for air. I threw it open further and crawled through it, onto the roof that covered the scullery below. The window was too small for the strapping farm lad who simply leaned out of it and watched me as I crawled, like an imp wreaking havoc during the witching hour, across the slate. I was nimble, despite my frail build, and as quickly as I could manage I reached the side of the house, where the roof met the sycamore tree that stood in the kitchen garden.

"I grasped for the branches, the leaves a mixture of fire red and burnt orange from the autumn season, and climbed into the tree. As I did, I saw the farm boy disappear away from the window from which I had escaped. Dinah appeared in his place, watching after me with horror, as if she had spied a devil dancing on her land.

"The young man was coming for me, scythe no doubt at the ready, yet I was seeping with a thrill that I had never felt before, spurred on by the kiss I had finally bestowed upon my love.

"By the time he was on the lane, bellowing after me never to come back, I was long gone.

"This new rush of excitement left me in a state of euphoric fury. It changed me. I became more brazen, and less meek. That winter I seethed over what had gone on, yet found myself smiling about it. I felt deliciously wicked. I wanted more. I started to feel an abhorrence for the life I had been dealt, yet relished it at the same time. I had freedom to be as awful as I wanted. I had already killed, after all.

"I began to despise everything about Fallows' Spinney and the surrounding land - yet I was forced to make my living from it. My heart ached for Jolette, who was dying in that back room at the top of the stairs. I thought of her and her daughter every single moment of every single day. Yet I hated Dinah. I hated her for feeling terror towards me - a man who had done nothing but watched her and bestowed her with trinkets her whole life.

"Word got out about the incident in the bedroom of The Spinney House. Dinah and the farm lad - whose name, I later learned, was Asher Harrod - told the other parishioners that they had found a bent old man lurking over Dinah's mother. They told them that the man had been frightful-looking and had called Jolette 'his love', and had kissed her with his dirty lips.

"The villagers realised it had been me that these youngsters were talking about. The parish became cold to me. The villagers stopped granting me their custom, refusing to buy firewood from me any longer.

"Yet, rather than retreat into utter reclusiveness, I found myself spurred on by my newfound taste for abjection and villainy. I would steal their wood from their outhouses so that they had no choice but to buy from me when I arrived at their doors on cold winter nights, suddenly without fuel for their hearths. I would charge them extortionate amounts for the firewood they so desperately needed during the frozen winters that gripped the parish, so as to spite them.

"They would call me the miser. The miser in the wood."

A tear rolled down Verity's cheek. She was deeply saddened by her companion's tale, and pitied him desperately. She pitied him, and Jolette and Dinah Clarke. And she felt that they were listening to this parable of despair alongside her. She felt they were stood in the backdrop somewhere, in the gloom of the room.

Verity felt herself holding her breath. She knew that this tale would only get worse. The so-called miser would end his life gasping for breath in the frozen earth. In some ways, he wondered if he had brought it on himself. He had killed a man, after all. But what had spurred Dinah Clarke on to murder him so brutally?

"Why?" she said, thinking aloud.

"*Why?*" he snapped back, accusatorially.

"Why did you die like you did?" she questioned.

"Because of *them*!" he seethed. "Because of Dinah Clarke and Asher Harrod!"

"But why did Dinah Clarke kill you?" Verity asked.

Tobe Thacker cackled - the laugh Verity had come to recognise was merely a mask for his anguish.

"She and Asher grew close, after that day they drove me from this house for good. I still silently watched the cottage from afar - mostly in the dead of night after that - but I saw Asher come back more and more.

At first it was in to check on Dinah and her dying mother, but then just to see Dinah. He was a comfort to her. He came to console her. She was, I gather, frightened of me, wondering if I would come back one day. Every time she climbed the stairs to tend to her mother she would wonder whether she might find me in the bed chamber, hunched over Jolette again, as if I were some hobgoblin visiting in the night to drink her blood. But as time went on, Asher became more than merely a friend to Dinah. They were both young, beautiful things. Their mutual, gentle affection turned into passionate love. And before long, she was carrying on much like her mother had with the dead Squire. They would rut in the parlour by candlelight, Jolette dying upstairs.

"They did not know, but I would wait for nightfall when they would pogue the hone downstairs, and I would climb the syca-more up to the window. I would creep in and sit vigilantly by Jolette, covering her ears so that she would not hear the depravity downstairs. It did not matter that even the scuffle around her had not woken her that afternoon the previous September when I had paid my visit. I felt that, even in her state of death-like sleep, she must know what was going on under this roof. And I wanted to protect her from it.

"Eventually, my duty of care came to an end. Jolette died in the summer of 1831 from whatever illness gripped her all those years. She died while Dinah was with child. Asher's child. She too gave birth to a girl later that year - Elodie. Jolette never knew her grandchild. It mattered not really, given that Elodie Clarke was yet another child born of sin. Asher never married Jolette, and he too died when the child was just a year old."

"How?" Verity asked.

The miser smiled at her from his chair, the glint of the Christmas lights reflecting off his solitary tooth.

"He simply stopped living," was his cryptic reply.

At this, a gust of wind curled around the house, causing it to creak louder than it had ever done since Verity had first walked through the door days ago. It seemed to scream, almost, like a frantic ghoul desperate to get inside. It felt as if every window sash rattled at the mention of Asher's death. The wind wailed inside the chimney stack, plummeting down the flue, echoing in the hearth and out into the living room.

The stack of birch logs by the fireplace then collapsed - the topmost wedge of wood falling to the floor, bringing with it several of the other silvery logs, clattering to the hearth rug and startling Verity in her dreamy state.

She still felt as if she were not fully awake, yet the sudden crash in the otherwise still and silent room was very real. She glanced around at the fallen logs, still with a sickly glean to them as if they were thriving with wet moss. Then she turned back to Tobe Thacker, whose face remained in shadow but was no longer smiling. His furrow had narrowed into a creased frown, his eyes stern and staring off to the side, as if looking at someone else in the room.

But there was no-one there - that Verity could see.

"Dinah raised Elodie alone," he said, through slightly gritted teeth, his voice a little more hushed, somewhat clandestine, as if what he was telling Verity was suddenly confidential. His demeanour changed, like he were an obstinate schoolchild trying to chat inside a quiet library.

"I still felt it my role to watch over them. Elodie was Jolette's kin after all. And besides, Dinah was an incapable mother. She had relied too much on Asher. And he was gone. Dead. She found it difficult and turned to the church.

"I believe she looked to God for solace, having experienced the death of her mother and lover so suddenly, one after the other. Yet I also believe she implored the church to help her raise Elodie. She swiftly enrolled her as a chorister. Partly, I believe, so she could send her off to be watched by the nuns at chorale practise several times a week.

"She also knew I was still around. The whole of Fallows' Spinney knew of the miser in the wood, and Dinah was the one with her very own horror story about me. The miscreant miser from the forest had come into her home, after all.

"Stories had, by this time, started to be told. Lies, of course. Tales. It seems I was already the stuff of folklore. The fools in the village were saying I was not a man, but a demon. I was a night-time hellion who would skip from roof-to-roof and peek in at the parishioners' children while they slept.

"Children began to come downstairs to their parents in the mornings and claim they had awoken in the night to see a pair of dark eyes glaring in at them from their windows. This was supposed to be me, you see. The hunched, wretched old man who used the drape of nightfall to do Hell's bidding.

"These fables prayed on Dinah Clarke's sanity even more. She became a verger for the church. Had it not been for her lustful past and her bastard child, I believe she would have fled Fallows' Spinney and spent the rest of her life in a convent, miles and miles away. Yet she had Elodie to raise.

"This mother and child became obsessively devout. They spent as much time as they could at the church, terrified of sinister forces. They were afraid of Satan. They were afraid of the creature that apparently lurked in the woods: me. They were terrified of this half-man/half-fiend who was in league with evil. I was a spectre, idling on the outskirts of the village, posing by day as a miser and roaming by night as a devil. I was a ghost before my time."

Verity had thought the very same thing, just minutes ago. Yet, she thought, the tale had taken another turn. Tobe Thacker had been two kinds of ghost: a loner, spectral in his utter insignificance to anyone else's life; but also a thing of legend - a malevolent gargoyle, chiselled into the tapestry of a parish thanks to God and His following.

Yet he was merely a man. A woeful, crestfallen, beggarly old pariah who had let his misfortune propagate and overcome him.

"I know I was a reprobate. A worm. I *know* that!" Tobe spat, clearly reading the pity and the disdain on Verity's face. "Yet there was still a glimmer of goodness in me. Part of me still loved Dinah and Elodie, having come from the loins of Jolette. And so I felt it best to show them this again."

Verity closed her eyes. She couldn't bear to hear it. What had Tobe done to these women - who had already talked themselves into being terrified of him - to make the pious and God-fearing Dinah Clarke snap?

He laughed again, brashly.

"It was not Dinah who took my life," he said, again as if he had read Verity's mind. "It was her bastard child. It was Elodie Clarke."

Verity's eyes widened as the name of the twelve-year-old chorister rang through the room. She wanted him to repeat himself, but she had heard him clearly already. His white face, shrouded in the darkness, glared back at her. He looked angry; yet relished in delivering the news, like a spiteful child implicating one of its siblings for breaking a precious figurine.

"It was on Christmas Eve, 1843. Fallows' Spinney observed, as it did and still does every year, Midnight Mass, after which the Clarkes returned here to The Spinney House, where Dinah put Elodie to bed, her head full of the prospect of candied treats and goose pie the next day. Her bedroom was the very same one Jolette had died in. The very same chamber I had kissed my love once, and only once.

"I wanted Elodie to have something from me. I had spent the yuletide carving her a trinket box, especially for Christmas. I wanted her to wake to find it at the foot of her bed.

"But Elodie Clarke had grown up dining nightly at the table at which my reputation as a miserable wretch was fed. She knew about the spirit with the dead eyes that watched children from beyond their window sashes. And so, when she woke that Christmas Eve to find me climbing through her window, she was of course afraid. And, in her fear, thanks to the stories that had been spun about me her whole life, she acted in malice. She leapt from her bed and she pushed me. I fell from the window."

Verity swallowed, her mouth dry as she listened to the ghost speak of the terrible series of events that had led to his death on the most sacred night of the year. At the hands, no less, of a child.

"What happened?" she asked, in a whisper.

"It did not kill me," Tobe continued. "It winded me, yes, but it had snowed that afternoon. The ground broke my fall. But I was an old old man by this time, and it certainly did me no good. Yet, looking up at the child - her face glaring down at me, ashen and afraid - was more painful to me than a thousand tumbles.

"We stared at one another for a long while. Neither of us moved. The cold wind rustled through the garden, otherwise silent in the dead white night. Elodie's mother, who had long gone to bed, did not hear the ordeal. The Spinney House remained dark and silent.

"The clock struck three at the village church and, for some unknown reason, it spurred me to rise from the ground and flee back to the forest, as quickly as my aged bones would let me.

"Yet that was not enough for little Elodie Clarke. I imagine she had a taste for what she had done to me. She had gone to battle against the miser of Fallows' Spinney. She had protected herself and her home and her mother from this wendigo that her village was so frightened of. She had maimed him. Yet she had not defeated him. She had not completed God's work.

"And so, that odious little girl - enraptured with the euphoria of the season - decided, that night, to carry out the most unholy of deeds. She escaped her family the following afternoon, her belly full of goose fat and orange sauce, and found me in my hut, tending my wounds from the fall. She found me where I was spending Christmas Day - and had spent the past fifty Christmas Days - alone.

"She crept in and she beat and bound me. I was weak and injured. She was a stocky young girl. It was no problem for her to accost me. I remember the way it felt to be sprung upon from behind, her little body like a spiteful cat clinging on to me with its claws. My aged and lovelorn bones could not fight it, and I could not withstand Elodie's wily youth-riddled strength.

"I was pelted with the rocks that she had gathered from the path that led up to my very own hut. My brittle wrists were locked together with coarse, threadbare string - the kind I used to secure my bundles of sticks. I was hauled through the frozen forest as the sun sank behind the trees that Christmas Day. I was dragged along the sodden meadows, soaked to the bone and grazed from the pebbly earth. And I lay, shivering, my cheeks resting on the dewy grass, watching from my spot on the ground as the grandchild of the woman I loved dug into the earth with the blunt shovel she had stolen from my wood store, creating the ungodly tomb in which I would die.

"I was made to stand, hands still clasped in the loose rope that any younger, stronger man would have been able to escape, and was pushed into the hellish ditch, where I would be left to rot.

"I managed to roll on to my back in time to watch Elodie use her clammy little hands to scoop up the slime and mud from the frosty ground and toss it down onto me.

"My stare met her's, as it had done the night before while I had lain on the snowy ground outside The Spinney House and watched her at her window. The earth fell into my eyes, my mouth. I could not call out, nor see. I was dumbed and blinded by this child, while her mother prepared crackling and dumpling stew for her before her bedtime at her warm home, as she buried me alive, believing she was working under the instruction of the Lord.

"As my dank catacomb was refilled by this rotten duckling, I gave in to the measly life I had been dealt. It was a fitting end. As the maroon sky faded from view, I prayed that the last of the earth would suffocate me sooner and that I might breathe my final miserly breath."

Verity was numb with despair. She merely stared at the ghostly creature before her, telling his tragic story. Her eyes, still stinging a tad from the tobacco smoke, now streamed. Her sight was blurred. The room felt as if it might suddenly drop, and that she might fall downwards into Hell itself.

"And imagine, now, in death, how it feels to know that Elodie Clarke did not pay for her crime," Tobe breathed, his voice low again.

Realisation came over Verity, as the tale came to a conclusion.

Dinah Clarke allegedly became particularly upset when her daughter, Elodie, 12, was announced as this year's so-called Solstice Sire (an honour granted to the child considered to be the most devoted chorister at The Church of Abbess Eunice).

Verity thought of the article she had read, in which Dinah had been taken into custody the following summer.

Dinah Clarke was later sent home to The Spinney House, where she was left with her daughter for the evening. Yet the local constabulary were later notified of a disturbance on the moors behind Miss Clarke's cottage. It was found that Miss Clarke had hiked to the top of the hill that overlooks her home, described by one of the investigating constables as "highly distraught, almost in a state of violent confession". She implicated herself for the death of the late Mr Thacker and was "constantly asserting that someone must repent".

Another chill slithered through Verity as she recalled the next part of the newspaper report.

As they attempted to placate the woman, other constables investigated her cottage, finding her daughter Elodie "calmly sat in the garden, wearing her Solstice Sire's crown of elder and oleander, hacking at the earth with a blunt piece of slate".

Verity felt sickened as she recalled how the events had come to an end. This girl's mother had taken the blame for what her child had done.

A court representative told The Stag following Miss Clarke's sentencing: "Dinah Clarke's distracted demeanour since last Christmas, which was attested for by a number of god-fearing witnesses from The Church of Abbess Eunice during the trial, paired with her behaviour at the Midsummer festival on the afternoon of June 24, and her attempted-defacement of Miser's Copse hours later, have proven a compelling argument against her. There are no other indications that anyone else was involved in this crime. The court has found that

Dinah Clarke is guilty of the murder of Tobe Thacker and she will be hanged at Horsemonger Lane Gaol on New Year's Day. Elodie Clarke will continue to be cared for by the church, before she is transferred to an orphanage."

Tobe Thacker shuffled forward in the chair, at last leaning into the dim light.

"You see, Verity?" he whispered, illicitly, as if he were speaking out of turn. "You *were* right to kill Tammy. Jolette birthed Dinah, and Dinah birthed Elodie. All out of wedlock. All sinfully. Elodie went on to kill. To kill *me*. Her mother took the blame. She died for her murdering daughter. All this, thanks to the brazen ways of the Clarke women. No good can come from women who conduct themselves thus."

He lent closer and whispered even more deeply.

"Like slatterns!"

He spat this word at Verity, yet it was not intended to spite her. His lacteal eyes shot quickly beyond her, into the corner of the room he had been distracted by earlier.

They were being watched, and Verity now knew by whom.

Little Elodie Clarke.

NEW YEAR'S EVE.
LAST YEAR.

Verity watched Tammy through the window of the Chelsea coffee house. She sat in the far corner, nursing a cup of herbal tea. She wore orange mittens and had a woollen scarf wrapped tightly around her throat.

There was a light breeze dusting its way around the West London streets that New Year's Eve. It was unseasonably warm for the time of year. It had been a dry winter - crispy leaves shuffling their way around the pavement at Verity's feet.

Tammy hadn't seen Verity who watched, in wait. She was staring vacantly into the cup she clutched in her mittened hands. She looked like a child in those bulbous orange things. But she was not a child. She was very much a grown woman.

As am I, Verity reminded herself, seething at the sight of her former-friend yet breathing out slowly to calm her emotions.

A few strands of her chestnut hair tickled at her cheeks in the tepid wind. She flicked them aside. A spot of warm rain landed on her lip. The breeze picked up. A woman walking past her erected her umbrella. Verity licked her lips and headed to the entrance of the café.

The door clinked shut behind her. Despite the close air outside, the wind moaned shrilly beyond the tall window panes of the coffee shop. She stood in the doorway and watched Tammy nervously sip from her nettle tea.

Tammy's eyes flicked across the room to see Verity had arrived. Verity stared back at her. Further droplets of rain began to spatter the glass behind her. The late-afternoon sky - flat and morose - had threatened to break at any minute. How apt, she thought, that this was the moment it had chosen.

With a sudden step, Verity walked across the coffee shop towards her friend, who awkwardly shifted in her seat, unsure if she should stand to greet her or to remain sat down. Before she could decide, Verity had dropped into the seat across the table from her. She stared directly into Tammy's nervous face.

"Hi." Tammy's voice was timid and weak.

"I thought it best we meet right away," Verity said sternly, sure to omit any form of pleasantries.

Tammy shifted in her seat and swallowed drily, watching Verity's expression before glancing away from her.

"Verity, look - "

"I'd like to speak first," Verity interrupted.

Tammy nodded and waited.

"I hear you had sex with my husband." Verity got right to the point.

Tammy looked down at her cup of tea. Verity watched her with wide eyes. Thirty seconds passed.

"Is that right?" Verity prompted her.

Tammy looked up and nodded, like a guilt-ridden child, without saying a word.

"Okay, so he was telling the truth," Verity affirmed, more to herself than anyone else. "And why did you do this?"

She spoke *at* Tammy, rather than *to* her. She was business-like and matter-of-fact. She was furious yet distraught all at once. In turn, this had plateaued into an almost robotised state. She felt a spite towards Tammy she had never experienced before. It was all aimed at her. Not Lochlan. She partially understood Lochlan. Partially. But she felt a venom toward Tammy; a venom she had wanted to spit at her at the earliest opportunity.

That moment was now.

Tammy spoke: "It happened shortly after - "

"After the argument at the office. Yes, I know that."

Verity wasn't there to mess around. She was there to get inside her friend's head, pick her mind apart, and then go.

"I want to know *why*, not *how*. He told me the logistics of it this morning," Verity said in her time-is-money tone, scolding Tammy.

At this point, a waiter approached the table.

"Can I get you something?" he asked without a flicker of interest, clearly irritable that he was being made to work on the afternoon of New Year's Eve.

"No. Thank you," Verity said without looking away from Tammy.

The waiter lurched away across the room and left the women alone at their table. The small moment of respite that the interruption had given them had allowed Tammy to formulate an answer to Verity's question.

"You seemed angry at me. And Lochlan was angry at us both. He wanted to talk about what happened and I suppose he sought a kind of solace in me because you weren't really speaking after what you did at the office party with that girl."

Verity allowed what could only be described as a snarl creep across her lips. She then stifled a laugh.

"*Solace?* Do you think that?" she asked.

Tammy looked anxiously towards the windows of the coffee shop. The rain had picked up rapidly. It was now running in slow streaks down the glass, as if it were slimy glue, sealing them inside.

"Lochlan was furious at *you* for goading me about Saskia," Verity went on. "Furious for encouraging me to believe that he and her were having some kind of affair. Playing on my doubts about our marriage knowing full well about all the issues we were going through about having a child. You preyed on our vulnerability. You encouraged me to think those things and to become so paranoid that I did what I did. Christ, it would have been more shocking if I *hadn't* approached that poor girl at that party and confronted her. You *made* me believe it.

"And Lochlan resented you so much for it that he *had* to seek you out to confront you about it. I told him to leave you out of it. I was the one who caused the scene and embarrassed him, after all. But he had to find you and ask you what the fuck you were thinking.

"He never wanted your solace. Or your compassion. Or even your comfort. That night you had sex with him was nothing to do with him needing you. Lochlan just wanted to take out his fury on you. *And* on me. On both of us. And you took advantage of that. He wasn't thinking. He fucked you out of hate - not because he wanted you. And yet you let it happen, despite being my friend. Was this what you wanted all along? To make me doubt him, pull him and I further apart and then get your own claws into him? I think you are so spiteful and jealous that you have no-one and we have each other?"

Tammy sat forward, tears in her eyes. "Yes!" She said.

Verity was startled by her honestly; although she had always known that this was down to her friend's jealousy. She also knew that the night Lochlan had gone to see Tammy to confront her he had not intended to sleep with her. The idea had come to him in a moment of madness - a way of taking his anger out on both women. On Verity for being unsure about motherhood and creating that scene at the office party; and on Tammy for feeding Verity the ideas about him and Saskia. Tammy had been a despicable friend.

Tears streamed from Tammy's eyes. She looked down at the table, and said weakly: "It's hard for me. It - it's hard."

Verity leaned in a little. "How *dare* you!" She hissed across the table. "How dare you even *touch* my husband!"

Tammy looked up from the table. Her cheeks were stained with tears - like the rain water that slithered down the café windows outside. Verity glared at her - up and down - and gave a dismissive tut.

"You're a whore." she jeered. "Happy new year."

Verity stood up, walked away from her, and headed outside

into the warm rain.

CHRISTMAS EVE. DAWN.

Verity sat up in the armchair, the faint sounds of rainfall waking her.

She gathered her bearings. She felt a little breathless. She wasn't sure where she was for a moment. She thought she might have been at home, in West London, in her living room. She turned her head briskly toward the dimly-lit Christmas tree that sat in the corner of the room by the staircase. It wasn't her tree. It wasn't her stairs. She remembered: she was in The Spinney House, Kiln Lane, Fallows' Spinney. And it was Christmas Eve.

The sound of rain petered out slowly. She glanced at the window. A slither of light crept through the murky winter clouds. Dawn was breaking. Lochlan had been in the copse for an entire night.

It hadn't been raining outside. She had dreamt about her confrontation with Tammy, last New Year's Eve. She had dreamt it precisely how it had happened - the water pouring from the skies outside the coffee house as she had called Tammy a whore. A taunting yet delicious pathetic fallacy, as if they had been dropped into a modern-day Bram Stoker novel.

She had evidently suffered a flashback; a moment of recollection, entwined in a fretful state of slumber. Not a dream; nor a nightmare. Something in between.

She could smell the scent of tobacco lingering in the air. With a jolt, she looked across the room at the chair in the corner. It was empty. No-one else was in the room. No-one she could see.

She turned to glance behind her at the corner of the room Tobe Thacker had kept his own eyes on during his story. Again - gloom, murk, nothing. No-one.

She wasn't certain whether Tobe Thacker had been real. She wasn't sure whether she had dreamt him, too; or whether she had been under some kind of hex, forced to sit, listen, and understand the story of the copse, the house, and the ghosts that haunted them.

But now, she was awake.

She pushed her hair back from her face. It was a little damp with sweat. She thought about the rain that New Year's Eve as the sound of the drizzle lingered in her ears from her slumber. That drizzle had developed into somewhat of a tempest that night, Verity recalled. She had gone home after leaving a weeping Tammy in the coffee house and spent a sombre night with Lochlan, not speaking at all for a long time before eventually dissecting their problems for the millionth time.

They had talked about whose mistake had been worse? Who had caused it? Was it all down to Tammy, or were they just as much to blame after all? Had there been problems in their marriage before that Christmas? Big enough problems that they had been able to bury them, allow resentment to swell and lead to Verity's outburst at the office and Lochlan's adultery.

Ultimately, they had spent the lead-up to midnight in silence, only realising the new year had arrived when they heard the distant sounds of cheering from a neighbouring house party, and the faint toll of a church bell.

They had met one another's stare across the living room and mutually seemed to agree that enough was enough. It had been a horrific Christmas, it was time to end the pain. They had risen and hugged as the rain hammered violently against the bay window of their home. In that moment, on January 1, Verity and Lochlan had entered an unspoken pact that the year ahead would be better. A decider.

And now - here they were: Verity conversing with the dead and Lochlan trapped in a shallow grave across the fields outside.

Verity was wide awake now; no longer in the murky state she had found herself in when the ghost had visited her. The tablet still lay in her lap, the screen black. The Christmas tree lights cast their eerie glow over the otherwise dark room. She leaned forward and stared at the armchair opposite her. Had she imagined it? Had Tobe Thacker really visited her in the night? Had her research of his death simply set her mind racing? Ghosts did not exist.

She thought about Tammy. That afternoon in the coffee house had not been the last she had seen of her, of course. They had cut Tammy out of their lives - until months later.

And now Tammy was dead.

Verity wondered whether anyone knew yet. They must do, she thought. It had been nearly a week. They won't have found her of course, but someone would have surely reported her to be missing.

Verity still wasn't certain at what point Tammy and Lochlan had had their night of faux passion. But she vividly remembered how Lochlan had been distracted in the lead-up to last Christmas - a time during which they had stupidly tried to occupy themselves by being overly sociable. Lochlan had harboured a residual fury towards Verity for what she had done at the office in front of his entire team. And then, a few days later, as Christmas had drawn closer, his demeanour shifted. It wasn't merely an anger at Verity - he seemed frustrated. With himself.

They had spent Christmas Eve - a year ago to the day - flitting between social events and ending up at Tammy's. Verity had clocked the tension between them, which she now knew to be a concoction of guilt and confusion and regret, impacted into one unbearable bundle that was festering within each of them like putrid cankers.

Christmas came and went. He drank too much. He was cold.

Verity and Lochlan had masked their issues as best they could by being on their best behaviour at his family celebrations and then her's. His mother had needed a hand with the green beans, and so Verity had jumped at the chance to vanish into the kitchen and keep her hands busy. Lochlan had gone to the pub with Verity's cousins on Boxing Day, which he normally tended to avoid. And no-one paid attention to this uncharacteristic behaviour because there were too many irritating children running around, high on sugar, distracting everyone with their incessant yammering about what Santa had brought them.

It was not until the days after Christmas that the truth had come out.

They had been at one of Tammy's post-Christmas-pre-New Year's dinner parties. She was always the hostess, it seemed; creating warm, inviting scenarios for friends and family, masking what Verity now knew to be unhappiness with bowls of steaming fettuccine and carafes of Châteauneuf-du-Pape.

It was at this dinner she had seen Lochlan watching Tammy. He had decided there and then that he could not bear it - or her - any longer. He was almost plotting as he glared at her, hating her for planting the seed of doubt into Verity's head about Saskia Warren weeks before, which had led to the episode at the office. He hated her for that, and for letting him fuck her that night a couple of days after, when he had turned up to confront her about it all.

He *was* plotting; plotting to tell Verity everything. Lochlan's bitterness toward Tammy became something he simply could not exorcise. That year, the Christmas limbo that comes afterwards became Lochlan's very own Abaddon. He was a man infected with despair.

New Year's Eve: a cursed day of the year. A day brimming with the promise of fresh opportunity, yet stained by the good and the bad from the past.

It had been last New Year's Eve morning that Lochlan had broken into a fit of tears in front of his wife. He told Verity what he had done just a few days before Christmas, with Tammy. He told of how he went to confront her for ill-advising his wife and then, weakly, allowed himself to use sex to get back at them both in one fell swoop.

Verity had been enraged, yet she partly understood. She had caused him pain in not wanting to have a baby when he so desperately craved to be a father. She had then gone and embarrassed him at work. She knew Lochlan had fallen sway to Tammy out of frustration and weakness. Sleeping with her had been a punishment to both women; it had not been out of desire. It was not simply masculine weakness, like it may have been with other men. Lochlan was not that stupid.

Both Verity and Lochlan had been equally devastated by the other. And, that New Year's Eve, after Verity had summoned Tammy to the coffee house to end their friendship, she and her husband decided that what had happened was either going to be their undoing, or trigger a fresh beginning.

They had opted for the latter.

They cut Tammy out, for good. Or so was the plan.

You killed her. You were right to kill her.

Verity couldn't help but smile at the thought of these words. Tobe Thacker was right. He understood her, because he understood her anguish. Only someone truly hurt by another human - or humans - could.

She had almost forgotten about Tammy over the past few days during their idyllic break in the country. But this man - this spectre - had reminded her that she had things to do.

She then thought again of Lochlan, still trapped in copse. He would have been squirming - like Tammy had done - like the worms that inhabited the earthy trench with him. She had to help him. She had to get him out. Tomorrow was Christmas. She had to finish her tasks before Christmas.

Verity sprung from the armchair, a little uneasy on her feet from her hours of sitting. Sitting, thinking, learning, understanding. She was still tired; yet her mind was racing, her heart pounding, all at once. She felt thirsty. She marched into the kitchen, her sudden movement and the thud of her walking boots on the wooden floor almost stirring the sleepy cottage into life.

She seized up a glass and poured herself some water from the jug in the fridge, devouring it ravenously and slamming the glass back down on the kitchen counter.

Out of the corner of her eye, in the living room, she noticed something lurking in the darkness. Verity stepped back into the doorway, squinting into the gloomy light. The curtains of the window at the foot of the stairs were drawn, yet slightly ajar, a slither of flaxen moonlight seeping through. Something stood there, in the corner, vaguely visible in the sickly strip of light.

A shape.

It was murky - smoky-grey, semi-transparent. The shape resembled that of a small, hunched figure, its shoulder catching the white beam from the window, remaining frigid in the gloom.

Verity frowned and leaned forward, attempting to look closer, without stepping back into the room. The hunched shadow remained still, mostly cloaked by darkness. Verity walked through the door to join the crooked smoky shape inside the living room.

"Is it you?" she whispered.

And then it moved.

With a sudden jolt, the crooked figure turned and faced her, suddenly presenting her with the sallow face of the old, toothless man, protruding from the darkness. The expression on his face was one of unbridled anguish.

Whether Verity and Tobe Thacker's encounter earlier that night, as he had sat across from her and told his dark tale, had been real or not did not matter. He was here now, stood before her.

The ghost did not utter a sound. The room was deathly silent, the only warmth coming from the Christmas tree in the corner. Even this bedecked symbol of joy seemed far from sanguine tonight.

The hunched shape lifted a spindly arm and pointed. A single, wilted finger stretched out. It pointed beyond Verity, towards the window, out to the moors - to the copse. *His* copse. Miser's Copse.

Verity's gaze followed the claw-like finger as it strained out from its shadowy nook in the corner. She stared out to Miser's Copse through the window at which the spectre was pointing. The clump of spine-like trees looked silver in the moonlight against the leaden sky.

It would snow, she thought. It will snow - and Lochlan is out there. And Tammy. What about Tammy?

Just for a second, she forgot about the creature lurking behind her like some kind of disfigured omen, arm still outstretched toward the copse. She was suddenly overcome with a rush of emotion - everything that had happened over the past year. And then, she felt purpose.

She ignored the ghost in the corner and seized up her coat and gloves, putting them on as she headed for the front door. She grabbed the keys to the Land Rover and, without looking back, left the cottage, the door closing firmly behind her.

The living room was left in silence.

From the shadows by the stairs, old Tobe Thacker moved. Hunched over, his face pallid and full of malice and sorrow, he trod quietly across the room towards the front window where he looked out at the pathway.

The faint morning light that was creeping across the sky illuminated Verity as she walked from the house, to the courtyard and the car, pulling her hood over her head, concealing her pitch black mane of hair from view.

DECEMBER 19TH.

The doorbell of Tammy's North London apartment was shrill.

On the night before the Tamblyns travelled to Fallows' Spinney, Verity waited for Tammy to come to the door. She wasn't as apprehensive about seeing her as she had thought she would be. A year of estrangement seemed to have done the trick. Absence had, however, made the heart grow somewhat blacker. Verity was not there to bury the hatchet. Not in the way Tammy thought, anyway.

The large panelled door of the third floor flat opened and there she stood. The year had aged her. Her face looked puffier, Verity thought. She was pale and a little fatter. Her body was shrouded in a baggy knitted grey cardigan, the sleeves flapping slovenly over her hands. Her face was pale yet her cheeks were flushed. She had been drinking, Verity guessed.

Perfect.

"Hi Verity," Tammy said. She was timid yet pleased to see her former-friend.

Verity swallowed her resent and beamed back at Tammy. And then she hugged her. Tightly; perhaps tighter than she had ever hugged anyone before.

Clearly taken aback at first, Tammy's body stiffened in Verity's embrace. Eventually she relaxed and sunk into the hug, wrapping her arms around Verity with relief.

The ice was broken.

After this, Verity stepped into the flat, before being invited. Tammy shut the door and the women stood in the middle of the living room.

It was a little untidier than how Verity remembered it. She hadn't been there for a year - almost to the day. Last time was during Tammy's post-Christmas dinner party, when she had watched Lochlan from across the table as he had seethed at the hostess through blurry, furious eyes.

That night, the house had been plushly bedecked for the holidays. A six foot blue spruce in the corner, scattered with pink and white lights, glass baubles glistening from every aquamarine branch. There had been porcelain jugs filled with winter cherry blossom, tall blazing sprigs of dogwood stretching from the bouquets casting spindly shadows around the room. Pillar candles burned on glassy candle-stands on the sideboards and in the centre of the dinner table, which had been adorned with damask napkins, sparkling silverware and rustic jars of condiments, ready for supper. Christmas cards were draped on string from one corner of the room, festooned across to the other.

This time, one year later, was a much sadder affair.

Tammy's normally hospitable home was sparse. A small table-top Christmas tree in a pot sat on the sideboard, decorated much more half-heartedly than any of its predecessors. No candles were lit. No flowers were on display. No boughs of holiday correspondence hung from above - just a few greeting cards sat on the dining table, which was barren and empty, save for a festive-themed salt and pepper pot in the shape of a pair of snowmen, which sat in the centre, next to a cream poinsettia in a terracotta pot.

The décor at Tammy's home this Christmas was a reflection of her year. She had upset many after what had happened between her and the Tamblyns. Many of their friends had sided with Verity over the matter, and, from what Verity had heard, Tammy had become intrusive and antisocial as a result.

This time last year she had been serving up a massive beef

tenderloin to a table of 12 friends, as they sipped on red wine and laughed merrily. It had been a tableaux of the season, despite the underlying troubles that Verity and Lochlan had been going through at the time. Now, however, the flat was empty, and quiet, and sad.

Good, Verity thought. Tammy had suffered the consequences. Yet it wasn't quite enough.

"It's honestly a little weird to have you here," Tammy said, playing with her hands beneath her baggy sleeves. "I didn't think you'd come back here again."

Verity smiled, sweetly. She glanced at Tammy's fidgety fingers. She had always been such a confident woman. None of this fiddling. She had changed.

"Want a drink?" Tammy asked. "I've been making Bloody Marys."

"Why not?" was Verity's reply.

While Tammy disappeared into the kitchen to fetch the drinks, Verity's stare rested on the French doors that led out to the small balcony.

"Can we go outside?" she called. "I don't know about you but I could do with some air."

"Oh. Yeah, sure." Came the dismembered reply from the kitchen. "I'll be there in a couple of seconds."

"Perfect," Verity whispered back, too quiet for Tammy to have heard.

The air outside was cold. It had been a freezing December afternoon and was a clear evening. The sky was a deep indigo colour, a streak of cherry off to the west, which seemed to illuminate the clean whiteness of the London sidewalk below.

Tammy lived on a quiet road, not much hubbub going on in the street. Verity could hear the faint hum of London in the distance – the noise of traffic, the odd car horn, a cackle from a woman somewhere who was probably stumbling home from a Christmas party.

Verity strolled out onto the balcony and stood somewhat authoritatively at the white balustrade. She looked down over the road below, lined with leafless trees that in the spring would bounce with pink blossoms.

Tammy stepped onto the balcony behind her, a tumbler of Bloody Mary in each hand.

"Here."

She passed Verity one of the drinks. She watched Tammy as she took a lengthy gulp from her own glass, the slice of celery that jaggedly stuck from the top of the tumbler awkwardly poking her cheek as she drank. She was nervous, and had probably downed another drink in the kitchen while she made these ones.

"Well. Cheers," she said, raising her glass.

Verity stared at Tammy for a moment before smiling again. "Cheers."

They clinked glasses.

"I'm a little nervous," Tammy admitted after another sip of booze. "I thought the last time I'd ever see you would be that meeting we had in the café."

Verity looked away from her, out towards the lights of the city.

"Yes. Well. That was the plan," she replied.

Tammy looked cautiously at her would-be friend. "So, what changed your mind?"

Verity let out a long impatient breath. "Oh, I don't know. I just wanted to see you," she answered, after a moment.

Tammy beamed at this. Verity looked back at her and mirrored her smile - only her's was far more wicked. She raised her own glass and took a sip. It was stingingly strong - more vodka than tomato juice.

"Verity, I have to tell you again how sorry I am for everything that happened last year."

She was slurring a little now.

"I know you are," Verity said, with faux sympathy; as if *she* were the one who should be sympathetic. She was, in fact, raging. But she had to keep her head.

Tammy went on: "Honestly, this year has been hard. I have

lost friends. I've put on weight. I haven't really cared as much about stuff. Like Christmas this year. I just can't be bothered with it. It feels different this year. I didn't even do my drinks this month for my colleagues."

Verity felt irritated. Poor thing, she thought. She's had to forgo hosting a little do. Never mind the fact she nearly ruined her best friend's marriage after fucking her husband. Never mind *that*. The real tragedy here is the fact that she couldn't play hostess.

"It's just been so hard for me," Tammy went on, turning a little to face the street, stumbling a little.

"I'm sure it has," Verity said, teeth gritted.

Tammy sensed the tone: "Oh, don't take it the wrong way. I know what you've been through is a lot worse."

Do you *really*, thought Verity? It occurred to her that other than a brief and rather vacuous apology, Tammy had only spoken about herself and how the whole episode had impacted *her*. This was her first response. And Verity wasn't surprised by it.

"I am so glad to see you. I hope we can just move forward. You, me, Lochlan. I want it to be how it was," she said, staring out at the frosty rooftops.

Verity smiled to herself. Lochlan didn't even know where she was right now. He wouldn't have let her come. He never wanted to see Tammy again, and that wasn't ever going to change. Verity hadn't told anyone about this visit, which had been the product of nearly a year of obsessively thinking about Tammy and how much she loathed her.

It had been Christmas that had done it: reignited the flames of vehemence she felt about her former-friend. She had attended Lochlan's office party last week; and, although this had been more than pleasant, with the incidents from the year before very much forgotten about by now, it had brought back memories. Vivid, unpleasant memories.

The whole reason she and Lochlan were going away to Fallows' Spinney tomorrow was to reconnect at what would forever be a troubling time of year for them. They had made much progress since then, but Christmas was too risky a time to stay in London after all that had gone on just twelve months ago.

Yet Verity had decided to do one last thing before they left.

That afternoon she had called Tammy and asked if she could come to see her. She had said she "wanted to talk". 'Tis the season to be jolly, after all.

And so here they were. This was it.

"I just hope, next year, this can all be forgotten," Tammy said dreamily as she continued to gaze out over the city.

She was deluded and insane.

Tammy turned around once more and stared at Verity. "Can it?" she asked, pleadingly. Pathetically. Her eyes red from the booze.

Verity smiled. "Yes."

Like an excitable little girl, Tammy grinned and raised her glass in a salute. Then, she turned fully around and downed the rest of the drink.

As she did, Verity extended her free hand, hovered the palm of it strategically behind Tammy's tilted-back skull, and with a swift, savage forcefulness, shoved her friend's head forward into the glass as it touched her lips.

A sharp "clink" as her front teeth rammed into the edge of the tumbler. The sound pierced the air. It cut through the night. It was the most satisfying sound Verity had heard all Christmas.

Tammy let out a muffled cry and she stumbled forward and began to spit and splutter. She covered her mouth with her free hand without turning around.

Verity watched her for a second - and then swiftly kicked Tammy's left leg, so that she stumbled against the edge of the balcony. She staggered clumsily, letting out a second whine, and reached out to steady herself against the balustrade. She was drunker than Verity thought; and she was blindsided enough to not know what was really happening. She fell against the balcony and slid to the ground, now facing Verity.

Verity stood above her for a moment, looking down with a

dark stare. Then she knelt and steadied her.

"Tammy, Jesus," she said, in a most convincing voice. "What just happened?"

Tammy, crouched down, looked up at Verity, her eyes dancing. Her hand was drenched in bright red blood. Her top lip was cut and fleshy. Her upper gum was sliced open. A shard of glass poked out from it. She still clutched onto the tumbler which was now lightly chipped, and dowsed in a bloody mess. Blood streaked down the glass where it had trickled from her mouth into the tumbler, contaminating the dredges of Bloody Mary that remained.

Tammy confusedly stared back at Verity. Her mouth and chin were stained with a red mess, which dripped down her neck, soiling her ugly jumper and splattering onto the white flagstone of the terrace.

Verity stared into Tammy's face and saw that blood sat thickly between her teeth – and one of them was missing. One of her canines had gone and there was a black gap in its place.

Verity was hit with a moment of pleasure and disbelief at what she had done. She gripped Tammy's shoulder, steadying her as she spluttered pathetically, disorientated. She looked frightened - although Verity was sure she didn't understand that this had been her friend's doing. Her eyes locked onto Verity's, pleadingly, before welling up.

"Did I trip? Or - ?" Tammy's voice gargled and choked on her own bloodied mouth. She sounded weak and distressed.

"I think you must have, yes," Verity cut in. "You need some water and a cloth."

"Please..."

Tammy was getting weepy. Verity couldn't help but play on it.

"And it looks like you've knocked out a tooth. But try not to panic. Be right back," she added cruelly, with relish.

She stood up and headed back inside. She went to the kitchen, hearing Tammy burst into tears behind her - a crumpled mess on the balcony.

The kitchen was bare. Mostly bottles of booze, mixers, plenty of ice in the freezer. Her exhaustive selection of cookery books and party planning guides, once pride of place, were now stacked on top of the cupboard, gathering dust.

That's what happens when you ruin other peoples' marriages, Verity thought.

She was feeling somewhat sinister and it disturbed her - yet she didn't stop. She was there to carry out a task; one that she had started, and must now finish.

She scooped some ice from the freezer and wrapped it in a tea towel. She grabbed the roll of kitchen paper and tucked it under one arm. Then she surveyed the kitchen countertop. She didn't know what she was looking for, but she would when she saw it. She scanned the items on the worktop: a cocktail shaker, an empty cake stand, a block of knives.

The latter piqued her interest. Too obvious, she wondered? Too cliché?

Too simple.

She continued to assess the instruments at her disposal. So many bottles of cheap wine. So many bumper value bottles of gin and vodka.

And then she saw it: the thing she had been looking for, without knowing it.

The crystal decanter she herself had gifted Tammy a few years ago when she had been promoted to senior account manager. It sat at the far edge of the counter, glistening in the sterile kitchen lighting. It was full to the brim with a plummy-coloured dessert wine.

This was what she needed.

Verity stepped briskly over to the decanter and seized it up. It was heavy, like she remembered it to be. It was heavy with or without liquid inside it. She took the stopper out of the decanter's neck and turned to the sink, tipping it upside down and pouring the wine out of it. It trickled into the chrome basin, the purple drink splattering up the sides of the deep sink and then swirling around the plughole, gurgling like Tammy had gurgled on her own blood-filled throat.

Verity left the top of the decanter in the kitchen - it wasn't needed.

She walked back to the French doors, to where Tammy still sat, sobbing on the balcony floor. She had her head in her hands. Verity placed the decanter on the edge of the balustrade, unnoticed by Tammy who was too wrapped up in herself.

"Here." Verity passed Tammy the icy towel.

She took it, sniffing, like a child.

"Thank you," she managed. "I suppose I need to go to the hospital."

Verity didn't answer, only passed her the roll of paper that had been under her arm.

"Get cleaned up," she said, uniformly.

Verity knew that she was going to do what she came to do. She had thought the sight of Tammy, in such a state, might melt her somewhat. But it was impossible. Verity was too full of venom towards this woman to be thawed. The image before her - Tammy, a mess, sat on the balcony floor, soaked in blood - made her despise her even more.

"Oh!" Tammy cried, looking up suddenly, blood and tomato juice around her mouth, tear stains on her flushed cheeks, the smell of vodka on her breath. "My tooth! We need to find my tooth!"

The way she said "tooth" made Verity smile. It came out "toof", as if she were a six-year-old. Verity stifled a laugh at the absurdity of the woman.

She needs putting out of her misery, she thought.

"Is that it? *There?*"

Verity pointed behind Tammy to the shadowy corner of the balcony. Tammy turned around promptly on her knees, still clutching the soggy tea towel to her mouth, and hunched over to look on the ground. As she did this, Verity reached out to the decanter perched on the balustrade. Efficiently, she wrapped her fingers around the neck of it and raised it.

She struck Tammy over the back of the head with it, as

cleanly as she had knocked her mouth into the tumbler minutes ago.

A clunk. Tammy fell forward, dropping the towel.

The decanter was such a sturdy thing that it remained intact. It hadn't quite done the job though.

Tammy was now on all fours, crawling, disorientated.

The task was unfinished.

Verity stepped closer to her former-friend and raised the decanter once more, bringing it down harshly onto Tammy's skull. And then again. Then a third hefty strike, smashing the makeshift weapon into shards over Tammy's head.

She lay face-down on the ground. Fresh blood oozed from beneath her straw-like hair, mingling with the spatters that had already come out of her mouth and were dotted around the stone terrace floor.

She lay dead - amid blood, juice, vodka, ice, shards of glass, a missing tooth and a jagged stick of celery.

It was a humiliating end, Verity thought. And quite fitting.

DECEMBER 21ST.
DAWN.

T he rook cawed outside the window, waking her.

Truthfully, Verity had barely slept. Her mind had been racing all night and when she had eventually slipped into slumber her dreams had been vivid and far from restful.

It had only been a few hours since she and Lochlan had arrived in Fallows' Spinney and to The Spinney House. Just a few hours since they had pulled into the driveway, entered the cottage, and felt instantly warmed by the seasonal décor and the homeliness of the place they would be spending Christmas. Just a few hours since they had made love in The Spinney House's bed for the first time.

Verity had fallen asleep and dreamt about it all: the journey from London, the sex. She had dreamt pleasantly about these things. Yet lurking amid it all was Tammy.

Dead Tammy.

Verity glanced over at her husband who was in a deep sleep. He had done the driving and was satiated from the sex. He breathed steadily next to her. He would be out for the count until at least Eight O Clock.

The rook that was perched on the sycamore tree outside

cawed again. The wintry first light of dawn snaked in through the thin gap in the drawn bedroom curtains. Verity rose from the bed and quietly trod across the room to the window. She pulled the curtain ajar and peered out. The moors were shrouded in a low-clinging film of smoky mist. The grass was wet, a few spindly bare trees poking up from the meadows here and there like skeletal scarecrows staring back at her.

She looked down towards the courtyard at the side of the house. The Land Rover stood where Lochlan had parked it on the gravel. On the top of it was the ski rack - long and thin, damp from the early morning dew.

Verity turned from the window. Wearing just her white nightie, she went carefully back to her bedside table where she opened the drawer, taking out the single key that was in there. She had stored it there shortly after they had arrived at the cottage, when Lochlan had been using the bathroom. She crossed to the bedroom door, giving her husband one last glance to ensure he was sound asleep.

Downstairs she donned her thick waterproof jacket, sliding it heavily over her flimsy nightie. She put the key from her drawer into her coat pocket, placed her sock-less feet into her hiking boots and tied her loose mane of hair back, out of her face. She seized up the car keys that had been left on the kitchen table and held them between her teeth as she, as carefully as possible, unlatched the heavy lock on the back door, pulling it open as silently as she could.

The freezing morning air nipped at the calves of her bare legs, the long coat only covering her from the knees up. She pulled the back door to, leaving it open just a slither, and removed the keys from her teeth, pressing down gently on the unlock button.

The orange lights of the Land Rover flashed, illuminating the flatly lit courtyard for a second. The car made its "blip" sound. Verity paused for a moment, eyes closed, hoping it had not been heard by Lochlan, who was astutely aware when it came to his belongings. Who could forget the time they had been in Italy, skiing, when he woke in the night, swearing blind that he had heard someone outside the chalet in the locked shed trying to steal his Black Crows Pack Daemon 2020s.

On inspection, it turned out it had been a curious ibex goat who had actually been no-where near the shed at all.

No movement from the cottage meant that Lochlan had not heard the car unlock. Verity could continue with her task.

She didn't need to start the Land Rover's engine, so this wasn't a concern. But she could not reach the roof rack without opening one of the car doors and placing one foot inside to give her a leg-up.

Verity crossed to the car and pulled open the passenger door, hiking herself up to reach the ski rack. She removed the lone key that she had put in her pocket and used it to unlock the straps that were secured around the casement. She endeavoured to be as quiet as possible, but knew it would be hard. The rack was already a cumbersome thing, and even more so thanks to what it currently contained.

She steadily slid the straps off the rack and secured her grip around the front of it, sliding it gently along the fixtures on the roof of the car. It glided along nicely, lubricated by the dewy slats. Still, it was heavy; and with all her strength, Verity pulled it from the roof, tipping it down the front of the car and sliding it to the bonnet. It was a two-person job, and that wasn't the way to remove it, but Verity had to do it alone. She had managed to push it up there on her own the night before they left for the trip, so she would manage now, too.

Once she had slid the rack along the bonnet and carefully down to the gravel drive, Verity placed it on its side. It looked like a coffin in the dreary morning light.

How apt, she thought.

She used the key to unlock the rack and steadily opened it.

Tammy lay inside. Not that anyone would know it was her, given that Verity had packaged her body up in black tarpaulin and secured it tightly with industrial tape. But sure enough, it was Tammy.

Dead Tammy.

Verity was no longer cold. She was perspiring. Perhaps she was anxious - after all, she was handling her murder victim; the victim she had killed on a North London balcony with a crystal decanter, wrapped up, taken home, placed in a ski rack and then taken to a remote West-English village, husband blissfully unaware.

Yet she felt calmer about the matter since they had left London and had arrived to the middle of nowhere. She realised that she wasn't concerned about Lochlan waking up and stumbling upon the scenario. Admittedly, it would be far more preferable if he just remained in bed during this task; but even if he didn't, she was sure he'd be glad to see the back of Tammy regardless.

Yet Verity and her husband had barely got through their troubles as it was. She was hoping she could avoid adding aiding and abetting to the list of issues in their marriage.

Verity was sweating from heaving Tammy's body in the roof rack as quietly as possible from the top of the car; and so she unzipped the large coat she had on and dropped it onto the driveway at her feet. Wearing just her cotton nightie and clunky walking boots, she hauled the makeshift body bag out of the ski rack and began dragging it along the gravel, around the side of the house, to the back garden.

The lawn behind The Spinney House was iced with the same smoky mist that clung to the surrounding fields. It swirled around Verity's naked ankles like eels in a shallow marsh. She clung on to the damp tarp as she dragged Tammy's corpse through the grass.

Verity had already decided where she would store the body. On arrival at The Spinney House she had noticed a coal store at the far end of the garden, overgrown with gooseberry thorns. She had purposely scanned the grounds earlier that evening, way before she and Lochlan had disappeared up to bed to make love. He had been replying to some emails at the time on the tablet, in the chair in the living room, where the web signal was strongest. Knowing he would be a while, Verity had stepped outside to do a turn of the cottage, spotting the coal store then. It was made of stone and was derelict: big enough to store a cadaver, yet small and tucked away enough (and entwined by brambles) for Lochlan to not pay it the slightest bit of attention during their Christmas break.

Reaching the coal store with the body in tow, Verity inspected the hole in the front of it. Ample room, she thought. With one final flurry of strength, she slid Tammy's carcass in its tarp along the grass, into the hole, and pushed it deep into the stony structure, until it was hidden from view.

Sure to keep it contained, she collected some of the residual shards of coal that lay at the mouth of the hole and pushed them inside, hiding the end of the tarp that contained Tammy's split skull underneath.

This was only a temporary fix, Verity decided. She would not leave Tammy here. But she had a holiday to start. And Tammy could wait for a few days. It was Christmastime, after all.

She retraced her steps through the soggy grass - parts of it flattened by Tammy as she had been dragged through it. Verity made sure no trail had been left on the lawn, kicking the squished grass blades back into their upright positions, getting rid of the tracks from the body bag. She was sure to do the same when she returned to the courtyard, shuffling the gravel with her boots so as not to leave evidence that she had been out in the night.

She closed and relocked the ski rack, hauled it - a lot lighter now - back onto the roof of the Land Rover, secured it with its straps, locked the car, picked up her coat and returned to the cottage. She hung up the waterproof, removed her boots and returned upstairs to bed.

She had been expertly careful in her task - apart from the smudge of coal that had gotten onto her white nightie. But Lochlan was up and out the following morning, leaving Verity a note on the pillow that he had gone into the village, without noticing anything at all.

CHRISTMAS EVE. EARLY.

L ike a witch making her Christmas Eve pilgrimage to cast a winter omen, Verity walked around the side of the cottage. Her hood was pulled eerily over her head, her face cloaked, her skin pale and drawn from the biting winter air and from her restless night.

She made her way to the garden, just as she had done at dawn on the morning after they had arrived in Fallows' Spinney. She trod softly through the frost-tinged leaves that littered the grass beneath her boots. The crunch of her steps on the ground were muted by the veneer of mist around her boots, thicker than it had been the other morning. This mist was more invasive. It seemed to be seeping from the sodden moors that stretched out on either side of the cottage garden. The dewy fog slithered from the wetlands, through the stone walls of the property, into the grounds, flanking Verity as she walked, like a sea fret suffocating a lost fishing boat.

She moved silently towards the coal store, like an apparition in the willowy haze, the occasional cry from the early morning rook that liked to sit in the sycamore tree at the side of the house, its caw penetrating the dense air.

On arriving at the coal store, an odour hit Verity. Tammy had begun to smell. It made sense, of course; although Verity had hoped the freezing air would slow her decomposition down.

There were light rips at the end of the tarp. An animal - possibly a fox - had tried to get at the body with its claws. Poking out through the torn plastic were tufts of Tammy's hair, still blood-soaked, but dry and stiff by now.

There was no time to be squeamish about this. Verity reached out and gripped the end of the body bag, pulling it out of the coal store and onto the grass.

A skinny spider scurried out from underneath the wrapped-up body and dashed across the grass, out of sight. The tarp was wet and slimy, cobwebs and woodlice on it from its four-day stay outside.

Not long now Tammy, thought Verity.

She didn't bother with the roof rack this time. Back at the car Verity simply opened the boot and lugged Tammy's covered corpse into it, clicking the button on the keys so it would close while she walked around to the driver's side of the vehicle.

She got in, started the engine and turned on the headlights. The windscreen wipers scraped slowly across the frost-covered glass. Verity turned on the heater and waited for it to clear. She glanced in the rear view mirror. She couldn't see the tarp back there, but the smell had travelled with it and was infiltrating the car.

She would clean it later, she decided.

As the frost began to thaw on the windscreen glass, Verity looked out over the courtyard wall at the moors beyond. It was a grey, dull morning, the fens lightly lit by the pale clouds that hid the rising sun as it crept from the horizon.

She saw him. He was stood on the heath, a black silhouette against the milky sky, a hunched, caliginous apparition - his waxen, bloodless face staring back at Verity with dark, sunken eyes. He was like an imp in a fable, caught roaming the fields in the early morning light.

Beyond him, at the tip of the hill, was Miser's Copse.

The ghost was too far away for Verity to see his expression, but she knew he was goading her - encouraging her. Not that she needed it. She knew what she was doing and where she was going.

The glass was almost thawed. Verity drove the Land Rover towards the cottage gates, out onto the lane. She thought about her journey with Lochlan, four days ago.

"You watch how she manoeuvres when we get to Fallows' Spinney," he had said to her, talking about the car.

"We're spending Christmas in a cottage," she had replied. "We're hardly going off-roading on the glaciers."

Of course, at the time, she hadn't known about Miser's Copse, nor about the readily-dug grave hidden in the trees. The grave that Lochlan was now trapped in. As they had driven along, with Tammy's corpse stored tidily in the rack just a few centimetres above their heads, Verity hadn't planned where she would dispose of the body.

But now she had the perfect spot.

"The place we're staying is pretty desolate. It's a mile or so from the village. The terrain could be rough," Lochlan had said.

Verity had brushed him off, as she always did when he tried to justify that clunky car. But now, at last, she was thankful for it as she pulled the Land Rover up to the metal gates off the lane, half-a-mile along from The Spinney House.

The gates opened onto the meadow that stretched uphill towards Miser's Copse. Verity got out of the car, glad to inhale the fresh air having been sat in the confined, gradually-warming vehicle with Tammy, while she rotted in the back. The gates were unlocked. The farmers out here didn't think about security, given how remote it was. And they surely weren't expecting any of the holidaymakers who came to stay at The Spinney House to bring with them the murdered bodies of their friends with the purpose of dumping them somewhere on the surrounding land.

Verity opened the gates. They squealed rustily - but no-one was around to hear it. She got back into the stink-filled car and drove carefully forward, onto the boggy field.

Steadily, Verity manoeuvred the Land Rover across the terrain, dodging rocks and low gorse shrubs here and there. The car bounced along the rough ground, grinding to a halt once or twice, getting stuck in the sloppy earth. Verity rammed her foot forcefully onto the accelerator, jimmying the galumphing vehicle out of the sticky soil and further up the hill.

Tobe Thacker was long gone from his spot on the field. Yet Verity knew he was watching her. From somewhere.

The sky still dim, the headlights from the car guided her as she became more confident at navigating her way over the terrain. Spurred on by the desire to see this through - and the stench of death that wafted from the boot - Verity drove faster. She was even enjoying this. She was beginning to understand the glee that driving Lochlan's beast of a car could provide. He would be delighted with her for this.

The incline beneath the car became steeper. The wheels stuck a little more. Verity stamped harder on the pedal. Miser's Copse was not far off. She could see the foreboding coterie of trees across the heath in front of her. The glare of the headlights bounced off the inscribed stone at the entrance to the path.

Nearly there, Lochlan, she thought. Nearly there, Tammy.

✠·✠·✠

Snow was coming.

Verity scanned the sky over the rolling moors from her spot at the top of the hill. It was a bitterly cold morning, not like it had been the other day when she had slipped from her bed and hidden Tammy's body in the coal store.

That morning had been wet and miry. It had been sodden and dank. Her task - in only a nightie and at an ungodly hour of the morning - had been far more arduous as she had transferred Tammy from the car roof to the coal store. It had been a burden. Verity had killed Tammy just the night before, after all. She had then spent the next day fretting somewhat. Admittedly, she knew what she had done and was pleased about it, but there was a constant tremor of fear and nervosa rattling through her on the day they had driven to Fallows' Spinney.

She and Lochlan, none-the-wiser, had travelled across the South-West, with packed cases and Christmas gifts stacked in the boot of the car and a dead woman contained on the roof of it. And so, yes; when the early hours of that following morning had finally come around, Verity had been nervy and fraught. She had woken to a damp morning outside, in a strange place, unsure of how soundproof their quaint Christmas cottage would be while she dragged Tammy through the grounds and hid her corpse.

She had succeeded, of course. But the whole scene had been dreary and onerous and terrible.

Since then, Verity had slowly settled into the reality of the situation. As she had enjoyed a mostly pleasant few days with Lochlan (ghostly visitors and a trapped husband notwithstanding) she had become oddly comfortable with what she had done. In truth, she hadn't given it much thought. It had flashed up here and there in her mind, but overall Verity had sunken nicely into the idea that it was Christmas - a merry time - and that she and Lochlan were fixing their marriage.

And yes: the fact that Tammy was dead helped her contentment. But Verity knew there was something about the scenario she had found herself in - Fallows' Spinney, Miser's Copse, The Spinney House - that was feeding her calmness.

It was soothing, mentally; but it was also infecting her, physically. Verity was freezing cold, yet she did not feel stiff. There was an inexplicable inner-warmth rushing through her. Her heart beat quickly and her blood pulsated throughout her body, accentuating the florid rash that still marked her skin and had, through the night, spread slowly around her frame.

And Verity's hair - now as black as ebony all over - although damp from the early-morning air as she stood at the top of the hill, was warm and sticky as it fell over her eyes.

It was this place, she thought, as she looked down towards The Spinney House. This place had consumed her. This place - that thrived on death and misery and revenge - had nurtured her.

She stood with her back to the Land Rover, which she had

parked at the edge of the copse, reversing it so that the boot met with the gap in the trees that provided the route back to Lochlan.

It was time.

Verity clicked open the boot. As the door rose up, the tiny orange inside lights gently illuminated the body bag, slumped across the back, which slid forward a little, half-hanging out of the car.

Verity started to drag Tammy out, but felt the sudden urge to stop what she was doing. She turned and glared out at the landscape around her again. The sky was steadily becoming lighter. It was low and leaden, charcoal clouds full of snow, ready to unload over the rolling fens that swept down from the copse at every angle.

Yet the sun was trying, hard as it could, to creep through. It was a battle - sickly light versus a dead chill. Both, Verity thought, were equally ominous.

She looked around as the dawn tried to break. Unlike the wet morning she had dragged Tammy's body across the lawn, the terrain was crisp and frosty. There were a pair of haphazard tracks that led up the hill from the lane, made by Verity's Land Rover. But since halting the car outside the copse and turning off the engine, the moors had fallen still and silent again. Early winter birds were whistling here and there.

Three rabbits hopped off to the west, halfway down the hill. A deer paused at the edge of the forest that stood between the moors and Fallows' Spinney, where children would soon be waking up, full of mirth, just one more day to wait until a visit from Father Christmas.

The deer - a fallow stag, undoubtedly - snapped its head around to glare at Verity. It was far away from her, right across the field, yet it fixated on her as she stood at the edge of Miser's Copse.

It evoked Verity's first morning at The Spinney House, when she had stood at the kitchen window, gazing up at the copse. When she had seen what she first thought was a stag, only to realise it was a small man. He had been carrying a bundle of sticks on his back, which she had mistaken at first for a pair of antlers. It had been the miser of the wood, Tobe Thacker. He had been watching her, knowing what she had been through and knowing what she had done. He had been sure that she was the one; finally, the visitor that he would be able to imprint on and infect with his own strain of misery.

And here she was; four days later, on Christmas Eve, back at the site of the miser's death, fresh blood on her own hands. She was there to, in a queer way, seal Tobe's tomb in its rightful spot.

The deer jolted off, into the woods.

Gone.

Verity blinked as a cold droplet tickled her eye. The flake of snow prompted her not to stall any longer. She turned and reached into the boot of the SUV and dragged the body out, letting Tammy fall with a crumbled thud to the icy grass. Verity pressed the button on the keys and the boot silently closed.

More flakes of snow. Some spattering onto the creased grey corpse-shaped tarp. Verity bent and wrapped her arms around the body and slowly dragged it into Miser's Copse, disappearing beyond the trees.

⊹⊹⊹

She wasn't sure what she would find inside the copse. She didn't know whether Lochlan was still in Tobe Thacker's ditch, whether he was dead or alive. He could have escaped, hitch-hiked back to London and be packing his things at their home, hoping never to see his wife again after she left him, overnight, in the hole.

She gripped at the tarp body bag, her fingers raw and frozen from the biting winter air. She was trembling a little under her coat as she lugged Tammy's rigid corpse along the narrow track, the sharp branches of the undergrowth swiping at her and catching on the body bag as she dragged it toward the heart of the copse.

It was dark under the trees, yet the breaks in the branches above allowed snowflakes to drift lightly onto her, dampening her black hair even more.

A bramble caught at her pale cheek as she stooped and pulled at the body. Yet, she continued on.

Verity had not seen Tobe Thacker since spotting him on the moor in the lights of the car; but she knew he was there, lurking, watching her in the copse.

His copse.

Any noise - the song of a robin or the bark of a fox - had been left out on the moors. Inside Miser's Copse it was silent, save for the scratchy scrape of Tammy's wrapped-up body being dredged along the stony, leaf-laden earth.

Occasionally, there would be a sudden sound of tearing as the tarp caught on a rock or a sharp twig. And it was becoming filthy - diseased by the dirty terrain.

Verity breathed heavily, but did not stop moving. Not even when the silver tape at the head-end of the tarp flapped open and revealed one of Tammy's eyes, placid, milky and sightless, staring back at her killer. Her friend.

Verity arrived at the clearing in the centre of the copse and dropped the tarp-covered legs of the body. She caught her breath a little and turned towards the dense shrubbery that led toward the site of Tobe's death. Toward Lochlan.

Tobe was there, hidden, watching. And without further thought, Verity seized up Tammy's legs again and pulled her along, moving backwards into the undergrowth of spiteful branches and low-growing gorse.

Verity could see the open grave. It sat, as it had done the day before, eerily lit this time by a sliver of dim light from the sky above that crept through a thin break in the trees. Flakes of snow trickled serenely down onto it. Some disappeared into it.

Onto Lochlan's body, Verity thought.

She felt a pang of joy, soaked in apprehension, dread and fright. She slowed down as she gained on the ditch, the crooked twiggy cross still protruding from the earth at its head.

She wanted to stop. She did not want to look. But she must.

Hanging from the cross was a wreath. It had not been there before and looked freshly-made. It glistened in the early-morning light; and the sprigs of fir and ivy adorning it were kissed with droplets of dew.

Verity let her head fall to one side, admiring the work of Tobe Thacker - for it was certainly made with his finesse. She smiled a little, yet the sight only fuelled the fret that now churned inside her.

Breathing sharply, Verity approached the edge of the hole, and peered cautiously into it.

He was still there.

She could just about see him. He was on his back, silent and motionless. It was dim down there, but the shaft of grey light that reached down from the break in the trees above lit up his face. His eyes were closed, his complexion white, his lips an eggy shade of blue, his mouth downturned in a thin, dolent crease.

A single tear rolled down Verity's cheek and into the tomb. The grave. Lochlan's grave.

She looked up, ripping her eyes away from the husband she had left to perish in the mordant earth. She wanted to weep, but could not. She knew what she would find as soon as she had seen the wreath, hanging mournfully from the spindly cross. She gazed at it and cocked her head, reaching out a pale, frozen hand, brushing her fingers through the sharp pine needles and ice-tipped twigs that decorated the wreath.

"So sweet," she cooed to herself, oddly thankful of the gesture from the miser in the wood.

Verity reached for one of the clusters of juniper berries nestled amid the foliage. She plucked a single pink berry from the wreath and raised it to her lips. It felt frozen and dense. Verity parted her lips - nearly blue themselves with the cold - and placed the single berry into her mouth. She bit down on the icy fruit and tasted the bitter juice as it laced her tongue.

And so, to work.

She turned around to assess Tammy's body, lying enwrapped in the grey tarp on the copse floor, battered from the elements, torn and muddy, a light stench seeping from the rips that had formed here-and-there.

Finish it, Verity thought to herself.

Bury her.

She bent to grab hold of the body bag again and hauled it in one swift movement to the edge of the open grave. She turned and glanced again at Lochlan, another jolt of despair rushing through her. She looked at his sullen, still face: the look of confused peacefulness that death affords you. Then she peered back at the body bag, on the edge of the hole.

She didn't want them to be buried together, like some sort of updated incarnation of Romeo and Juliet. Lochlan didn't need to be plagued by Tammy in his place of decay. He didn't need to fester into the earth while lying face-to-face with the woman who planted the very seed that ruined his life. All of this was because of *her*.

Verity kicked the body bag at the thought of it. She grunted as she did so, the body only slightly wavering by the force of her foot. She did it again. And again. She laughed as she did it. She enjoyed doing it. It hadn't been enough that Verity had split open this woman's skull with a crystal decanter. It hadn't been enough that she had stolen her body and brought her out to the middle of nowhere, at Christmas, leaving her in a coal store before dragging her through this copse. None of it was enough.

Verity crouched down and grabbed at the tape that sealed the body bag. Her freezing cold hands shook as she fumbled, trying to rip it open, trying to get to Tammy. She was too numb and flustered. She screeched with frustration.

She tipped back her head in annoyance; and when she looked back at the tarp again, she spotted the eye - Tammy's eye - still glaring at her through one of the tears in the plastic.

Fuelled by her rage, Verity looked frantically around her, spotting a sharp rock on the ground. She reached for it and dropped firmly to her knees. She bent over the body bag, slotting the rock into one of the tears and slicing it open with one swift motion. The ripping sound pierced through the silent copse and Verity pulled at the plastic to prize it apart.

She was hit by the smell of death. Tammy's body was rigid, her face affixed into a tight, twisty grimace. Her hair was crawling with lice. There was a slimy coating of dew lining the inside of the plastic, and clusters of maggots here-and-there. Her clothing hung from her skin wetly, and there were patches of open, sore rot on her chest and neck and one of her forearms.

But it was her face - *that* face - that Verity could not bear to have looking at her. However dead the eyes, however vacant the stare.

She wrapped her cold hands around Tammy's even colder neck and held on, closing her fingers tighter and tighter. The skin was loose, and she could feel it peeling off the deteriorating flesh beneath. She could feel Tammy's bones under that. She felt sick by it, yet carried on trying to squeeze the life out of something already dead.

She released her grip and pulled her hands back from the corpse, brushing her own black hair from her face.

A sound. Probably a pheasant. She glanced around.

She saw him: Tobe Thacker was now stood in the dark trees beyond the bent cross that marked Lochlan's grave. He was silent. He was not grinning. He looked stern. His face was one of authority.

She didn't look at him for long; but, his eyes on her, Verity spun on her knees and reached for the rock that she had used to slash open the tarp. She seized it in her hand - slimy and craggy to touch - and raised it above her head, her breath producing cold bursts of air as she did so.

She closed her eyes and brought the stone down onto Tammy's dead face. She screamed as the rock smashed into the expressionless look in Tammy's eyes. She dug it into her friend's creased, flaxen skin. She hacked at Tammy's features, turning them into mush, fuelled by her despair and hate.

Had she found Lochlan alive still, Verity knew she wouldn't

have done this. Had Tobe Thacker's power - fed by his own intoxicating mixture of anguish and bitterness - not overcome her, she would have contentedly kicked Tammy's body into the hole and left her to decay further. But Lochlan was dead and Tobe was present.

She leant her weight onto the rock as it burrowed into Tammy's face, squelching and moulding it into something new.

And then she was done. She did not want to see Tammy - however unrecognisable - ever again.

Spinning on her knees, still clutching the now-flesh-riddled rock, Verity crawled away from the body and away from Lochlan's grave. A few yards along the frosty earth, she stopped - and began to dig.

She hacked at the crumby earth with the rock. Beneath the frosty surface it was cruddy and loose and easy to burrow into. She dropped the rock and used her nails to pull apart the ground, making progress unnaturally quickly. Her fingers began to bleed, but she didn't care. She managed to grip large clumps of soil and remove sizeable slops of mud from the ground, tossing them off to the side.

Still frozen from the sharp December air, Verity was determined to complete her disgusting task; and, knowing she was being watched from the trees by the miser of Fallows' Spinney, her eyes did not leave the earth in front of her. She ravenously dug at the copse floor, through leaves and twigs and stones, seizing up massive mounds of supine mud and throwing them anywhere she wanted, occasionally using the jagged rock to create a deeper trench in the soil.

She was dirty with black earth, her wet hair in her eyes, snowflakes drifting around the scene, falling on Verity and onto Tammy's caved-in face as she lay on the copse floor behind her killer-turned-undertaker.

Before long, Verity had made enough headway that she was able to climb down, below ground level, still on her hands and knees, and mine deeper and deeper. She was as determined as a vole, furiously weaving a nest in the autumn wheat ahead of the encroaching winter.

Verity began to hack at the innards of the bespoke cavern. She pushed loose mud up the sides of the ditch walls so that it would spill out over the top. And soon, the little trench became a ditch. And then the ditch became a shallow grave.

She stopped, her hair now matted with clammy soil, her face stained with mud, her fingers bloody from scraping at the rough terrain with her bare nails. She pushed her sodden hair away from her eyes and exhaled slowly.

Enough, she thought.

She had purposely dug the hole at a slight incline, so that she could hike herself up out of it. It was nowhere close to the depth of Lochlan's - the one he had been unable to escape and had died inside. Verity was able to stand and hop lightly out of this second ditch, digging her left boot into the hole's walls, hauling herself upwards out of the mouth of the bespoke catacomb.

She allowed herself a moment's rest as she bent over, catching her breath, cold wisps of air coming from her lips. She twisted her neck and stared across the ground toward Tammy's body, and her deformed face.

Finish this, she thought again.

Verity walked slowly over to Tammy and grabbed her legs once again, pulling at the tarp with its great slash in it exposing the corpse inside. Bits of Tammy's face fell off and remained on the leafy ground as Verity lugged the body towards the freshly-dug hole.

Reaching the edge of the ditch, Verity looked down into what would be Tammy's final place of rest. It was rocky and muculent.

It was perfect.

With an exhausted sigh, she rolled Tammy's body into the trench. It thudded onto the rocks, lifelessly. It landed face-down, Tammy's hacked-off features hidden from view. Her corpse was still half-covered with the tarp, her bedraggled, filth-encrusted hair still crawling with maggots, almost moving like a black mass.

You killed her.

The words rung in Verity's head. It was as if Tobe Thacker was whispering them into her ear.

Verity spat into the ditch.

"Rot!" she whispered.

And then, a voice: "Verity?"

It was a man. It was a young man. It was the voice of a living thing - not the gargling, distant voice of an aged ghost.

She feared turning around. She feared that it was Lochlan. She knew it could not be; yet, that *voice*. It couldn't be. Surely, it couldn't.

Verity closed her eyes and turned slowly.

"Verity?"

Again, her name was spoken. It was clearer now that she had turned to face it. It was a young voice, yet somewhat pained.

It couldn't be.

She opened her eyes.

Lochlan stood before her. He was filthy, his eyes pallid, his skin taut and a languid shade of pale blue. Frost tinted his eyebrows, dirt sat in crumbs at the corners of his mouth. Dried red cuts dotted his cheeks and hands, his clothing torn here-and-there. He stared at her, confused, aggrieved and unwell.

And his hair - it was jet black. Blotches decorated his collarbone and creeped a little up the back of his neck. He was infected by this place too.

She closed her eyes again. He was not real. He was a spectre, like Tobe Thacker. Yet this thought startled Verity. Tobe Thacker *was* a spectre, but he was also very real.

Whether or not Tobe had joined her in the living room of The Spinney House the night before was still murky in Verity's mind. She was still far from certain as to whether or not the miser of Fallows' Spinney had been with her, or simply infiltrated her dreams and told her his story. It had been too cloudy an experience for her to be sure. But she knew for a fact that he had knocked on her door a few days ago; that he had watched her from the kitchen window as she had lapped up the sunlight, naked, the next morning; that he had stood in the moonlight at the foot of the cottage stairs, pointing out to the copse, instructing her; that he had been watching her from the moors and now the trees. He was a ghost, but this did not make him any less real.

And so: was Lochlan - dead Lochlan - a ghost too?

The sudden sensation of a hand firmly gripping Verity's wrist prompted her to open her eyes again with a jolt and a sharp intake of breath.

Lochlan was holding onto her, his bruised, soil-encrusted hand quivering. This was not the unsteady rootlessness of a ghost. Ghosts, Verity had learned, possessed fortitude. Even frail old Tobe Thacker - he was not meek. He was sinister and oddly puissant, despite his physical degeneracy.

No. Lochlan was alive. He had survived all this. Yet the eyes that looked back at Verity were somewhat soulless and exhausted. And his hair - ebony. She knew that her own eyes would be staring back at her husband with the same vacuity. They had both been infected by the land, the history of the land and the ghosts that trod the land.

"Verity?" he asked for a third time, as if unsure whether it was her, his words laced with pain.

"Lochlan," she breathed, her own voice quavering. "You're... I thought you were dead."

He frowned. He looked like Frankenstein's Monster - pieced together with cruddy bits of skin and left to roam the wilds of the countryside, unaware of who or what he was, or how he came into being.

She wanted to embrace him, but couldn't seem to bring herself to do it. She was in too much shock. He was too unsettled and delicate. They were both too bedevilled with whatever force had blighted them to engage in such acts of natural, human affection.

"Dead?"

"Yes. You looked dead. Down there."

He turned and looked back at the ditch, still confused and

somewhat manic.

"How long was I down there?"

She wanted to lie to him, but didn't: "All night."

His brow became furrowed, muck flaking from it as his forehead moved with confusion.

She went on: "I thought you had frozen to death. There was no way I could get you out without... '

She stopped speaking, hit with a tremor of her own confusion.

How *had* he gotten out?

Lochlan had been lying stiffly in the trench not two minutes ago, as trapped down there as he had been the afternoon before. As trapped as he had been all night and morning - up until that very moment.

"How...?"

She tried to ask him, but couldn't formulate the words. She began to feel dizzy. Her gaze dropped a little. He noticed, his own bemused expression becoming one of concern. Verity staggered on her feet, the sudden fatigue hitting her. Over the past twelve hours she had hiked up a hill, been knocked unconscious, hiked back down the same hill, stayed up all night while being force-fed stories of death and adultery and hate, driven a heavy car across an unruly moor, lugged a dead body through Miser's Copse and then dug a shallow grave with her bare hands. She was exhausted.

Lochlan reached out with both hands and steadied his wife as she lost her footing, her eyes staring widely beyond him to Tobe Thacker's ditch.

"Verity, steady," he said, suddenly a little more capable.

She looked from the hole, back into Lochlan's concerned eyes. "How did you get out of there?" she asked, nodding at the ditch.

The look of confusion returned to Lochlan's face as he turned to also scrutinise the hole, then back at his wife.

"He helped me."

Verity's own eyes burned into Lochlan's, desperate to understand what he was talking about.

"Who helped you?"

"The man."

"Which man?"

"The old man."

He could not mean Tobe Thacker, she thought. But she knew he did.

"He held out the cross and used it to pull me up," Lochlan went on.

"What cross?" Verity asked, her head swimming with disbelief and unease and fright.

Lochlan let go of his wife's arms and turned to point: "There."

Indeed, the makeshift headstone made of sticks that formed the shape of a cross and had Tobe Thacker's name scratched into it lay on the leafy ground. The sharp end of it looked like a stake, as if freshly carved to slay vampires with. The fresh wreath that had hung from it now lay on the cold earth, at the head of the ditch. It no longer looked pristine and sparkling. It appeared to have died. The juniper berries were grey and shrivelled, the pine twigs slack and bare, the winter leaves brown and ailing.

"But... that cross was just there, in the ground." Verity stated. "The wreath was on it. It was green and... "

She trailed off as she realised that it was not the news that Tobe Thacker had saved Lochlan that was bothering her. Nothing that had happened in the last twelve hours had truly been logical. If a frail old ghost had been able to somehow extend that spindly cross down far enough to reach Lochlan for him to grip onto - so be it. If a frail old ghost had, despite Lochlan's weight, been able to haul him out of the ditch, then Verity could accept that.

What bothered her more was that he had only now chosen to do it.

She had seen Tobe Thacker in the copse shortly after Lochlan had fallen the previous afternoon. But he had run from her; before thrashing her over the head with his bundle of sticks. What was it that he had wanted from Verity to put her through the hours that followed?

Had it been Tammy? Had he wanted Tammy - a whore - finished off and buried in the copse as some kind of vengeance for his own tragic past? Was Tammy some kind of sacrificial token? Tobe Thacker believed, in his delusion, that the Clarke women had betrayed him with their acts of passion. Was Tammy's murdered corpse being used by this deranged spectre as a totem of justice?

And then, as if on cue, as the thought of Tammy entered Verity's mind once again, Lochlan's eyes fell upon the second grave. Tammy's grave.

He brushed past his wife and took a step to the edge of the hole that Verity had worked hard to dig. He peered down into it, his body still trembling in the crisp December morning air.

Verity did not speak. She did not know what to say. She simply waited.

"Verity?" Lochlan uttered, without turning. "Verity - who...?"

His voice trailed off, but he continued to scrutinise the body in the ditch at his feet. Having fallen face-down, Lochlan had to stare hard at the corpse. He would have had to do this if Tammy had landed on her back too, thanks to her deformed face. Lochlan could have climbed down and spun her over, and still not been able to identify that it was Tammy, given that her features were scattered about the copse floor in fleshy fragments.

Yet, somehow, he knew.

"Tammy?"

The word impaled Verity. It was the way Lochlan said it: with a disbelieving, appalled horror. Every single time her name had been spoken by her husband (which had been rarely over the past year) he had referenced Tammy with such disdain.

Now, he said her name with disgust - but it was not a disgust at Tammy herself; he was disgusted at the state he was seeing her in. And he knew who had done it.

Lochlan turned around and looked at Verity. He was aghast.

"Is that *Tammy?*" he asked, one trembling finger outstretched in the direction of the hole behind him.

Verity nodded, silently.

Lochlan stared at her for a moment longer, realisation seeping across his face, and said: "Did you...?"

She nodded a second time.

His expression morphed into one of utter misgiving. He had never looked at her like that. Not ever. Not that time she had made the comment about his cousin's baby being ugly. Not when she had thrown away the misshapen sweater his beloved grandmother had knitted him before she died, without realising how he had adored it. Not the time she had dented his old Jeep with the wrought iron gate when they spent that weekend in Scotland at Stoat's Crook. Not when she had behaved appallingly at the Christmas party and screamed at Saskia Warren.

No - this was a look of odium that she was seeing in her husband's face for the first time. And it angered her.

"Verity. What the fuck?"

She was suddenly filled with rage. It wasn't the rage she had felt toward Tammy that had coaxed her into killing her. This was fury.

"Pardon?" she asked, coldly.

"You heard me."

Both of them were suddenly not the shocked, vulnerable pair they had been a minute ago during their unprecedented reunion. He was bold and assertive once again. The blueness was slowly fading from his cheeks and a pink blotchiness was taking over.

"I killed her, yes." Verity said this as if Lochlan had merely asked whether she'd done the dishes while he'd been entombed overnight. "I killed her for what she did to us. And then I brought her here. And then I buried her."

He stared at her, open-mouthed.

"Well - I was *trying* to bury her," Verity corrected herself, noting that Lochlan's subsequent resurrection had interrupted her from filling in the grave.

His eyes danced darkly as he calculated precisely what his wife had just owned up to; and how she had done it so blithely.

"What's the matter?" she asked, impatiently. "Aren't you happy she's dead?"

He stared wildly at her. "No!" he said.

Verity's own eyes darkened.

"What?" she spat.

"Of *course* I'm not happy she's dead," Lochlan elaborated. "Are you out of your fucking mind?"

She did not care for this tone.

"Pardon?" she said again, curtly.

"I asked you if you're out of your *fucking* mind?" he said again, rather deliriously, taking a step towards his wife.

She chewed on the inside of her lip, irritated.

"No, Lochlan. I'm not."

"You have *murdered* Tammy," he argued back at her.

Using Tammy's name seemed to send a jolt of furiousness through Verity. It seemed so strong that she took a step backwards. Lochlan was glaring at her with revulsion. It seemed that despite her ridding the world of Tammy for *them,* he didn't appreciate her efforts.

"You *hated* her!" Verity barked, offering a dose of rationale.

Lochlan's mouth tried to crawl upwards into a smile - a brief flash of disbelieving amusement at the logic Verity was trying to serve him with. But it swiftly fell back into a gape of disbelief.

"I might have hated her, but not enough for you to do *this*!"

He was somewhat screeching now. He was coming across hysterical. He had awoken after a night close to death in a ditch, on the morning of Christmas Eve, and had been helped by a ghostly old man, only to learn that his wife had executed the woman he had slept with last year out of spite. Not only this, his wife was not as much as flinching about it.

His eyes began to glass over with tears.

"My god! Tammy..."

He said it as if he were apologising to her on Verity's behalf. And this would not do. Verity's veins seemed to pulsate with menace towards Tammy. And now Lochlan too. Both of them disgusted her. She felt hot. Her face felt flushed and suddenly prickly. She shook her head a little.

She stepped back, treading on something.

The cross.

Verity noticed a shape out of the corner of her eye, beyond both of the graves, in the trees. It was a crooked, half-hidden figure, dark amid the gloom. She caught the flash of a drawn, pale face. Just for a second she saw dark eyes, a thin grin. The hunched shape of Tobe Thacker then glided out of sight, deeper into the thicket of trees.

Lochlan's face was now stained with tears. Blood, mud and tears.

"I've got to get her body out of there. And back to London."

He was mad, Verity thought. Quite mad.

Lochlan turned as if he would climb into Tammy's grave, but then stopped and looked up at Verity.

"Help me. You can make this right," he said to her.

She merely laughed at him. This reaction angered Lochlan. He seemed to suddenly pulsate with the same strain of fury that was coursing through Verity's body. His eyes blackened and he launched himself towards his wife.

"You did this! *You!*" he raved, running towards her, away from Tammy's grave. "*You* listened to her! *You* confronted Saskia! *You* embarrassed me! *Your* behaviour made me fuck Tammy!"

He marched toward Verity. She was now standing closer to the mouth of the original hole in the ground. Tobe's grave.

"*You* didn't want to have a baby!" he seethed, taking a final lunge towards his wife. "All of this was *you!*"

The malice practically spewed from his mouth with these final words. But Verity was quick to silence him.

With one swift jab, she plunged the peaked end of the cross into her husband's stomach as he advanced on her. He fell quiet, his ferocious eyes bulging with surprise and pain.

She held the sharp stick in place, twisting it a little as it impaled Lochlan's torso. It had been easy enough to do, given that his jacket had fallen open as he had dashed towards her. She had quietly picked the cross up from the ground behind her and hid-

174

den it behind her back when he had turned to retrieve Tammy's body, before turning back to his wife. And now, it was imbedded inside his gut, a gurgling sound exuding from his widened mouth.

He looked at her - still appalled. Even more so. She glared back at him, her own eyes glinting with the early stages of tears.

He stumbled forward, his weight on her, held up by the stick that had lanced him. The intensity in both of their expressions waned. They allowed each other one final look of sorrow and anguish and love. And then Verity loosened the grip on her spear, stepping aside and letting her husband fall forwards, into Tobe Thacker's grave once again.

He landed on his back, the cross sticking out of his stomach at an awkward angle. His face was achingly sad. Verity could see that Lochlan's final thought had been one of regret. Regret that it had come to this.

This was truly Lochlan's grave now, Verity thought.

She looked up towards the trees. No-one. She was sure that Tobe Thacker was lurking, but he remained hidden.

She stepped back from the hole, standing between where Lochlan and Tammy's bodies each now lay. It was a poetic end, she thought. They had both betrayed her; and although Verity had only brought one corpse to Fallows' Spinney with her that Christmas, she had known she and Lochlan would not return to London together in the new year.

She set to work: first on Tammy's grave. She scooped up the masses of wet soil that she had tossed in every direction as she had dug the hole. She retrieved the earth and dumped it back into the ditch, onto Tammy's body. She kicked stones and leaves and twigs into the hole in an effort to fill it up as swiftly as possible.

As Tammy's maggot-infested corpse disappeared, disguised beneath the ground by earth and rubble from the woodland floor, Verity began to cry; for Tammy, for what had happened between them and for how this had all ended.

Then she returned to the first grave. It was time to bury Lochlan.

This was a far more arduous task, given that the ground had fallen in with her husband when he had first become trapped. And so, as the morning of Christmas Eve passed, Verity worked, exhausted, to collect rocks and branches from around the copse. She dug new mounds of muck to throw into the hole, slowly covering Lochlan's body, packing him firmly into the earth.

His body disappeared, and with it the spindly cross that protruded from his abdomen. She watched as the scratched words "Tobe Thacker" vanished from sight as she filled in the tomb. She watched this, as Tobe Thacker watched her, from his silent vigil beyond the trees.

Robins sung and the snow had stopped falling. Silver-yellow sunlight spilled in through the boughs of the trees as Verity undertook her task.

Lochlan's still, sorrowful face was the last part of him she would cover. She wanted to look at him one final time.

As the birds whistled in the branches above, the sun flickered across the copse floor. Entrenched several feet below, Lochlan's face had begun to look somewhat serene. His mouth downturned, without emotion; his eyes shut.

And then, they opened.

Verity wasn't sure whether she was imagining it or not. Surely, she was. But as Tobe Thacker reappeared at the edge of his hiding place in the trees, the sunlight slicing through his smoky visage, she knew she had to complete her task. The miser stared back at her with purpose. There was not a glimmer of the macabre grin that he usually wore on his lips. He glared at Verity, cold and draconian.

And so, shunning any temptation to try and save her husband again, Verity scooped the last of the earth into her hands and dropped it into the grave, where it fell into Lochlan's face.

The soil landed in his widened eyes, slowly covering them from view. His mouth seemed to open a little as Verity let more gravelly mud fall into the hole, filling the narrow gap that she could now see between his parted lips. Silently, she buried him alive, just as Elodie Clarke had done to Tobe Thacker, in the very same spot.

┼┈┼┈┼

Verity sat behind the wheel of the Land Rover, still parked at the edge of Miser's Copse.

She had taken her time picking her way out of the copse, stopping occasionally to steady herself, starting to wane from the exhaustion.

Robins and pheasants and rooks sang from their hidden spots in the trees and undergrowth. Shafts of sunlight - now golden as the morning had brightened - trickled through the bare branches, dancing on the pure white snow that had fallen onto the patches of ground not canopied by the firs and the pines of the copse.

Verity had finally broken free of the dense cluster of trees. There had been no wind across the moors that sprawled out in front of her. It was eerily silent out there, save for the odd call of a winter bird or the bleat of a sheep.

As she had returned to the car and sat herself behind the wheel, she took in the mass of white that now surrounded the copse. Thick snow covered the meadows. The tracks the Land Rover had made in the earth were now flanked by a blanket of sparkling whiteness. She could see The Spinney House down the hill. It too was snow-tipped, like something from a Christmas card.

She had been numb, she realised; for the past few hours she had been somewhat drunk on whatever force had overcome her. And other than the flash of emotion she had experienced when first reunited with Lochlan, Verity had, beyond her own comprehension, enjoyed her unearthly doings.

Yet it had merely been thanks to the hold of whatever hex had infected her. Now, it was leaving her, seeping from her bit by bit. And suddenly, she could move; she felt light again. She was

177

no longer paralysed and rigid. Her skin, reddened from the rash, felt clean once more. She was free; and with this freedom, a rush or despair, sorrow, shame and fright burst from her.

Verity's eyes streamed with tears: for her dead husband, for Tammy, for the Clarke women, for Tobe Thacker.

She clutched the steering wheel of the Land Rover and she screamed. It pierced the bitter air that languished on the moors around her, and slithered into Miser's Copse, like a siren. It slipped between the naked boughs of the snow-tipped trees, across the frozen earth and along the path of the copse. Her scream slid through the undergrowth and dissipated amid the barren limbs of the pack of black trees at the top of the hill.

⊹⊹⊹

Verity didn't bother locking the car as she walked, exhaustedly, around to the front door of The Spinney House. She even left the windows slightly open in an effort to banish the stench of death and dirt from it. She did not want it following her back to London when she drove home - if, indeed, she would do so. She had not thought about what would happen next.

Around the cottage, the moors were peaceful and unmoving - yet far from serene. There was something in the air, she thought. It was as if something had followed her from Miser's Copse, back to the house, and was lingering in the low mists of the fens, watching her.

Not Tobe Thacker's ghost. Not a ghost at all. This time it was a semblance of some kind; the sort of veil that shrouded Miser's Copse. That odious covey of trees from which she had driven back were laced with ill-feeling and misgiving. Each branch dripped with a sour, ominous despair. The earth beneath the copse, with its tangled web of snaky roots, beat with malice. Miser's Copse was a portent, a harbinger, of woe.

And as Verity had left the copse, this malice had crept through the meadows and followed her down to The Spinney House. And so, on the most exciting day of the year, the en-

178

ergy of Christmas Eve was now dissipated by wretchedness and gloom.

She hobbled past the front window of The Spinney House and noticed a shape inside the living room. It looked like a man. A tall, broad-shouldered, young man. Verity felt a rush of eagerness and joy. Was it Lochlan? She understood, in that moment, how much she loved her husband.

But, of course, the room was empty. No Lochlan. No man at all. Just Verity and her exhaustion, playing with her mind. Lochlan, after all, was in the ground, choked to death on soil and bleeding out, into the dirt that now entombed him.

He had joined the haunted earth.

Inside, she looked around the front room. The greenery that had bedecked the cottage was dead. The boughs of pine that snaked up the banisters were ruddy and threadbare, yellow needles on the floor. The bay leaves above the fireplace were brown and stiff, poking out from the dead conifer garland. The Christmas tree itself was limp and dry, its boughs hanging lifelessly, like bony arms, weighed down by its ornaments. The angel at the tree's summit was crooked.

It looked sad.

Verity closed the door. It was stiller and quieter in the cottage, with the door shut, than it had been out on the moors. But in here, she was no longer being watched. Whatever presence she had felt in the house the night before was either gone or hiding. It had not been banished - she knew that. Tobe Thacker would never be banished. The Clarke women would forever remain - their tragic lives clinging on to every brick in the house, haunting it. But the glaring cloak of doom that slathered the frozen fields outside where at bay, for now.

For the first time in hours, Verity felt a little safe. Contained. The living room was laced with a gentle white early morning light. Christmas Eve morning.

She climbed the stairs and went to bed.

CHRISTMAS EVE. NIGHT.

Verity slept.

From the moment she fell into the bed she slept like the dead. Slept like Tammy and Lochlan and Tobe Thacker. Slept like Jolette and Dinah and Elodie Clarke - one dead from disease, the other hanged for a crime she did not commit.

The third's fate was one Verity had not learnt. The murderous child had likely been sent to an orphanage, grown and released into the world where she had probably lived a long, healthy life. Perhaps a life in which she had gone on to kill again. Or perhaps she had had the life her mother and grandmother had been denied - with the love of a husband and the joy of a happy family.

Verity woke, groggily.

The blackness of the back bedroom was what had stirred her from her hours-long slumber. She had slept deeply, dreamlessly, and missed the entirety of Christmas Eve. The cottage had remained still and silent all day. There was no need for anyone to come out this way, away from Fallows' Spinney, on Christmas Eve. No postmen to deliver last minute Christmas gifts to the holiday cottage; no farmers at work; no other vacationers for miles.

The meadows had remained eerily quiet throughout the day

- as if the birds and the deer and the hares had sensed that they should stay as far away from The Spinney House as possible. As if the aura that had seeped down the hill from Miser's Copse and now lay stagnantly on the fields and on the lawns of the cottage was a deterrent, warning anything from coming closer.

Verity had spent Christmas Eve truly alone, sleeping upstairs, under the moss-tinged slated roof of The Spinney House - a place of sorrow and death disguised as an idyllic Christmas hideaway. It was as if Verity had been allowed, finally, to rest. She had earned it, somehow.

That Christmas Eve, not one chaffinch had sung on the chimney top of the house, nor a vole scurried amid the undergrowth of the walled gardens outside as the sun had risen and then fallen again over the flanking fields.

Yet eventually, long after nightfall, Verity stirred.

She woke to pitch-blackness. Lying still, a light flurry of panic rose in her. Despite her colourless sleep, thoughts of Lochlan and Tammy in their graves had been lurking at the back of her mind; and as she opened her eyes to pure darkness she felt for a second that it was she that had been buried alive in the ground.

But no. A sliver of pearly moonlight crept through the window across from her bed; and as Verity's eyes adjusted to her surroundings, she recalled that she was one of the only living things in or around The Spinney House.

She lay for a few moments, on her side, strangely calm. Dread had trickled through her as she had remembered where she was and what she had done, yet it paralysed her. She felt hopeless and had no reason to get up or to even move.

Then she felt it: something at the foot of the bed.

It was a brief, gentle movement; the sensation of someone sitting by her covered feet, on the edge of the bed, the soft sound of the bedspread creasing under the slight weight of whoever was now there.

Verity held her breath. She remained still, staring at the window across the room, the panes frosty, the sky outside clear save for one feathery wisp of cloud, stars twinkling as they should do on Christmas Eve.

There was then a sensation of someone shuffling a little by her feet. It was gentle and unassuming. Yet Verity felt frightened. She could hear the soft sound of breathing, just a few feet from her at the foot of the bed.

Was it Tobe? No, she deduced. This felt like another presence altogether.

Thoughts of Lochlan and Tammy entered her head; thoughts of their cruddy corpses, zombified, maggot-infested, having clawed their way out of their graves, slowly skulking down the snowy hill, creeping in through the front door, up the stairs and now sitting at the end of her bed, watching her with hatred for what she had done to them.

But no; this was not a revenant nor a hellion. This was something less unsightly, but still truly terrifying. The presence may well have felt lighter and less oppressive, but Verity knew she was being visited by a terrible thing.

Slowly, she turned her head and looked down the bed.

A little girl sat there. She was a heavy-set child, of about twelve-years-old, in a cornflower blue dress. She wore a Solstice Sire's crown on her head, made from elder and oleander.

This was Elodie Clarke.

The girl - Tobe Thacker's killer - smiled. Her dress was pretty - yet dirty and torn. She busied herself with something in her hands. She was turning it over and over, examining it, contentedly inspecting it.

Catching the slither of moonlight from the window, Verity saw that it was a little wooden box.

I wanted Elodie to have something from me. I had spent the yuletide carving her a trinket box, especially for Christmas. I wanted her to awake to find it at the foot of her bed.

Verity remembered Tobe's story of the night he crept into Elodie's bedroom - the very same room Verity had slept in all day - and left a gift for the child. And now, here she was - visiting Verity in the night as if she were Ebenezer Scrooge and Elodie were the Ghost of Christmas Past.

Verity craned her neck as far around as possible without moving too abruptly, watching Elodie's face, half-lit in the moonlight, grinning almost smugly at the box as she twirled it in her hands.

Then, she stopped. She looked up, towards the bedroom window.

Verity knew what would be there, yet she too turned and looked across the room.

Through the glass was the ghostly white face of Tobe Thacker: the miser of the wood. His eyes were on Elodie, who glared back at him. His face was sunken, his mouth downturned sadly, his expression affixed in a state of longing and remorse. He did not move. His body was not visible. It was as if he were merely a disembodied face, glaring in through the frosty pane.

Elodie looked back at him. She was not afraid. She was no longer smiling. She glared at Tobe, her eyes narrowed, her mouth pursed. And then, after a moment more, she placed the wooden box onto the bed beside her and stood. She stepped slowly across the room and up to the window.

Verity lay still, the bed covers up to her chin. She watched as Elodie Clarke faced Tobe Thacker, a thin sheet of glass separating them. They stared at one another, silently. It was tense and unsettling. It seemed to go on for minutes and minutes. It felt so uncomfortable to watch that Verity shut her eyes and waited.

More time passed. No sound was made. She remembered Tobe's story of how Elodie had pushed him from the window, in an attempt to defeat the so-called spectre of Fallows' Spinney.

Yet when she opened her eyes again, Verity was met with no-one. Neither Elodie nor Tobe were at the window any longer.

She let out a long breath; it felt like the only breath she had allowed herself to take since she had first felt the little girl's body sit down at her feet. Slowly, she unravelled herself from the bedclothes she had been wrapped tightly up in and rose from the bed. She scrutinised the window where, moments ago, one ghost had stood and peered out at another.

She trod carefully into the spot that Elodie Clarke had been; the spot from which this child had pushed Tobe Thacker off the roof on Christmas Eve 1843.

She felt a chill. It was either the thought of the little girl's brutality or the residual presence of Elodie in that very spot. Or perhaps it was merely the cold crisp night air, seeping in through the thin glass pane of the little cottage window.

Verity reached out to the latch. As she did, she caught her reflection in the glass. Her hair was no longer black. It had returned to its natural tawny shade. She smiled, pleased at this sight.

She unlatched the window, pulling it open. Freezing air instantly invaded the room, yet she pulled it wide and stepped forward, poking her head through and peering down into the cottage garden.

There was an early morning fog shrouding the snowy lawn below, thick and dank. She looked down at the ground beneath the window - the place Tobe Thacker would have landed and lay, staring up at Elodie, having fallen at her hand.

He was there; not strewn on the snowy grass, but stood, his neck twisted awkwardly upwards, his face glaring at Verity. He was smiling - the same grin she had come to know so well over the course of the days prior. He looked at her, nasty and gleeful.

Verity lifted her leg and placed one foot on the low sill. She gripped the edges of the sash and hauled herself up, stepping through the window. She stepped onto the mossy roof, bringing her other leg through. She stood outside on the roof gables, the freezing air snapping at her in the light breeze under the clear inky sky.

Tobe Thacker watched her from below, his mouth open with delight, his one ugly tooth protruding from his sickly gums.

A giggle.

Elodie Clarke.

She was no longer in the bedroom. She was now also outside, in the garden. Verity looked across the lawn and saw her, sat, lightly cloaked by the fog. She sat on the sparkling snow in her mucky blue dress, her crown still atop her head. She was hacking at the snow, trying to get at the earth below with a jagged wedge of slate. She was making a hole in her spot on the blanket of white that covered the lawn. She was digging out the mud underneath and staining the virginal ground in front of her with muck. Defiling it.

Verity stepped forward, toward the edge of the slate roof. It was uneven, and laced with glistening frost. She stumbled a little.

The moonlight shone down on the foggy garden. The sycamore tree at the side of the house along the roof jerked suddenly in a brief gust of icy wind, which howled lowly as it blew. Verity's foot slid slightly on the slate tiling. Tobe Thacker gasped with delight beneath her, his eyes flashing darkly in the silvery light, enjoying her peril.

Elodie Clarke ceased her vigilant hacking at the snow. She too looked up at the roof, watching Verity, her face sullen and firm. This was not the face of a child; not the face of innocence. Verity shuddered to think what this girl would have become, had she survived past her youth.

And then the church bell chimed. Three O Clock. Three rings. The same as the night Tobe Thacker had died. The three rings that had prompted him to retreat back to his shack in the wood, where Elodie would later hunt him down, kill him and bury him on the hill - as Verity had done with Tammy and Lochlan hours earlier.

Lochlan. She thought of her husband as she stood on the roof under which they had hoped to save their marriage. The cottage she had travelled to with him, the corpse of their friend bound and locked in the rack on top of their car.

As the bell from the village struck a third time, Verity felt Tobe Thacker's stare on her, willing her to do it.

Tammy had been missing for days. The car was soaked with the stench of her. The Spinney House lawn was besmirched with Tammy's remnants from where she had been dragged out of the coal store. The tracks of the Land Rover were ploughed into the snow on the fields and, when that melted, the grass beneath. The path through Miser's Copse was littered with bits of tarp and flakes of rotting skin and dried blood. Parts of Tammy's face was scattered about the site where two shallow, freshly-filled graves had been dug. Verity's nails had been in the loose earth just hours earlier.

She had had her revenge on Tammy. She had killed her husband. Tobe Thacker had used her to spread his virus of anguish. And now he stared up at her, darkly, goading her to conclude the whole affair.

She may as well join the rest of them, Verity thought, stepping off the roof of The Spinney House.

CHRISTMAS MORNING.

Haunting vocals floated through the crisp morning air - the choir of Fallows' Spinney ringing in Christmas from The Church of Abbess Eunice. The joy-filled voices drifted through the village, the woods, along the lane and across the moors, sparkling with snow in the morning sunshine.

The song was the Coventry Carol.

Lullay, Thou little tiny Child, By, by, lully, lullay.

It was a clement day - unusual for December 25. Robins chirped in the spindly trees that poked up here and there from the snowy meadows. A rook swept across the ice-blue sky from the woods, landing on the sign at the edge of the lane that read "The Spinney House", indicating the charming cottage at the foot of the hill.

This poor Youngling for whom we sing, By, by, lully, lullay.

A hunched-over figure walked silently across the heath, towards the copse that rose from the snow-tipped hill. The old man carried a bundle of sticks on his back as he trod slowly across the white ground.

Then woe is me, poor Child, for Thee, And ever mourn and say; By, by, lully, lullay.

In each of his hands, the crooked man held two of his brittle sticks. They were both tied at the tops with smaller twigs, each one forming a long, thin cross. He slowly trudged up the hill with the pair of makeshift cenotaphs, gaining steadily on the wizened murder of trees ahead.

Charged he hath this day; All children young, to slay.

At the edge of Miser's Copse, Tobe Thacker stopped and turned, glaring out at the rolling fields that slunk down towards the wood and the village beyond.

Families would soon be feasting on meats and cheeses and sweet wines, their homes bedecked with brightly-lit firs, handsome wreaths, bright chrysanthemums and dancing candles. Children full of mirth and zest as they unwrapped their gifts - oblivious that they lived in a village guilty of burying its macabre yuletide past as close to Hell as possible.

His face grave, unsmiling and full of solemnity, the ghostly miser turned and disappeared beyond the gnarled, snow-laced trees.

THE STAG: NEW YEAR'S EVE EDITION

RED CHRISTMAS! THREE BODIES DISCOVERED IN SUSPECTED TRIPLE-HOMICIDE AT THE SPINNEY HOUSE AND MISER'S COPSE

Police have cordoned off the copse overlooking Fallows' Spinney after three bodies were discovered in the area yesterday, December 30.

Authorities were notified by a Mr. Timothy Bleak, owner of holiday home The Spinney House, Kiln Lane, on the outskirts of the village, when he attended the cottage yesterday morning.

Gloucester-based Mr. Bleak visited the cottage after receiving a call from a local farmer, who noticed that the front door of the property had been open since at least Boxing Day. Having unsuccessfully tried to contact the renters - a young couple visiting from London for the Christmas week - Mr. Bleak travelled to the property to discover the house was indeed unlocked, the belongings of his renters still inside, but no-one present.

Mr. Bleak noted that the couple's car was parked in the yard, windows open, keys inside the house. He also came across blood in the snow in the back garden, underneath an open bedroom window.

On arrival, the police noted that marks in the snow suggested something had been dragged off the grounds and up the neighbouring hill, towards the small thicket at the top - Miser's Copse.

Further investigation has uncovered footsteps, tyre tracks, blood and human remains, found sporadically between The Spinney House gardens and Miser's Copse.

Inside the copse, further remains have been located on the forest floor. Initial signs point to at least two separate sets of remains, from what appears to be two females.

Police announced yesterday evening that three shallow graves have been located inside the copse, each marked with a makeshift cross made of woodland sticks. Hung from each grave was a freshly-made wreath.

The entire area has been announced as out of bounds to both the public and the farmers who work on the neighbouring land. The area has been declared a crime scene. The families of the missing couple have been notified and the graves are set to be exhumed today.

It is being treated as a triple murder or a murder/suicide. There are also reports that it could be a ritual or copycat killing. The latter refers to the fact that Miser's Copse is the site of a similar burial, which took place on Christmas Day 1843, before the copse was there.

Detective Superintendent Rachel Dornan addressed the findings and the initial rumours that there is a copycat at large in a statement last night.

"Fallows' Spinney has a rich centuries-old history and, at Christmastime especially, is known for its tragic past. And, while the past should always be reflected upon, it is not to be dwelled on.

"I would strongly urge those speculating about the circumstances of these recent findings not to panic nor to draw conclusions until the proper investigations have been carried out over the next few days.

"We cannot confirm nor deny yet whether there are human remains in the shallow graves we have come across, but this information will be made public once exhumation has been carried out.

"Until then, my advice to the community is this: Please be diligent, do not allow local lore to muddy your logic and enjoy the last few days of the festive season. Happy New Year."

THE END

ACKNOWLEDGEMENTS

I'd like to thank Sandra Parsons, Literary Editor at the Daily Mail, for her encouragement, and for introducing me to Luigi Bonomi at LBA Books Ltd.

Many thanks also go to Luigi himself, and Hannah Schofield, for their invaluable guidance as I wrote – and re-wrote – this novel.

To Clare Povey also for her notes on the manuscript, which were extremely glowing, for which I am very thankful.

Thank you also to Felicity Blunt and Rosie Pierce at Curtis Brown.

ABOUT THE AUTHOR

Andrew Bullock works as a TV and entertainment journalist for MailOnline. He has also written for Vanity Fair, YOU magazine, Gay Times, Metro, The Express and Attitude.

Before becoming a journalist, Andrew dabbled in script writing - sitcom and feature film - eventually deciding to bunker down and concentrate on his love for gothic literature. And so Miser's Copse was born.

He works in London and lives in Berkshire. Much like Stephen King has dog Molly aka The Thing of Evil, Andrew has cat Cali aka Princess of the Macabre.

Miser's Copse is his debut novel.

Printed in Poland
by Amazon Fulfillment
Poland Sp. z o.o., Wrocław

59575802R00115